Hunting the Reaper

J.R. Carlson

ISBN: 978-0-578-71680-0

DEDICATION

This book is dedicated to the entire realm of mortals who enjoy fantasy and adventure. May the winds of change and the tides of adversity always shift in your favor!

CONTENTS

i

CONTENTS

Hunting the Reaper

ACKNOWLEDGMENTS

Thank you to all my family and friends who have been so supportive throughout the years! Also, a big thank you to Terry Brooks, J.K. Rowling and Joseph Delaney for the countless hours of entertainment and inspiration throughout the years!

PROLOGUE

Mortals have many names for us. Some call us ghosts, spooks, wraiths and phantoms. Here in the Immortal Realm, we refer to ourselves as spirits. Everyone here used to be mortal...until we died of course. Now we are merely flexible forms of highly refined matter who can walk through walls and travel at incredibly high speeds in ways that mortals would never even dream of...but I'm getting ahead of myself. This book is about the Grim Reaper or simply called, "the Reaper" as we refer to him here in the Immortal Realm. Older souls often refer to him as the "Soul Collector."

There have been many tales told about the Reaper within the Mortal Realm. The majority of them are false accounts commonly used to frighten or excite those looking for a thrill or a chill within their desperate mortal lives. I begin writing this book in hopes that one day a mortal soul will find and share it with the rest of the Mortal Realm. It may bring much needed hope to those who are wondering why so many unnatural deaths have occurred and what is currently being done to stop them from happening. Many who have passed into the Immortal Realm have done so long before their time was up. This book contains many untold secrets that have been hidden away for centuries! Of course, there are a number of reasons untimely deaths can occur. Many of them are due to poor life choices, accidents, angry people looking for revenge, war, natural disasters, diseases and famine are among a few of the many reasons this can happen. This book is not about any of those things! No, this is about the supernatural deaths that have happened to perfectly healthy people for what seemed like no reason at all. Sure, the Reaper can still collect the souls of the sick and injured. In most cases, you mortals will blame the sickness or injury as the cause of death. We here in the Immortal Realm don't blame you for thinking this way. After all, we were once like you.

Many attempts have been made to stop the Reaper from collecting the souls of the innocent. Although new efforts are continually being made, it might not be long before every mortal is completely destroyed within the Mortal Realm of existence! I don't want to cause a sense of panic or fear but the Reaper has been causing unnecessary death and destruction for far too long now! I know you're not able to see him with your mortal eyes and you'd be surprised to find out just how much spiritual damage can affect you on a physical level. Sudden bursts of discouragement or quick waves of doubt could easily be labeled as being "overly dramatic" or blamed on "catastrophic events" in your mortal lives. However, you'd be surprised to learn that spiritual weapons can harm the soul even more than physical ones. There is even a rumor floating around the Immortal Realm about a weapon so deadly it could destroy an immortal spirit! Of course, it might just be an absurd rumor since we have already died once. I mean, a spirit can't die again, right? Well, it hasn't happened yet. Thank goodness for that! The truth is...

CHAPTER 1

THE GATHERING

The clock struck midnight and the chimes began to sound. Jimbo looked up at the giant grandfather clock staring back at him. It was time to go. He looked around the room from where he sat at his small wooden desk. A large roaring fireplace lit up the entire room nearby to where he was sitting. Tall rolled up scrolls leaned against the stone walls throughout the room. Glowing lit candles sat on his desk and on top of the many small bookshelves lining the walls of his study area. The light of the full moon shimmered through a small glass window into the study room of his home. This was his favorite area in the whole house. He could read and write books until the end of time if he didn't have other responsibilities to attend to.

He dipped his feathered quill back into the small bottle of ink on his desk and gently closed the book he was writing. "I'll have to finish this later," he thought to himself. Time always seemed to move faster than he was comfortable with and he always got nervous trying to get anywhere on time. He grabbed his small travel bag lying on the floor next to him and began filling it with various objects he would need for the journey ahead. Since he was a spirit, he had no need for items such as food, water or even an umbrella. No, he had no need to eat, drink or even keep the rain off himself. His human needs died with his mortal body. More pressing concerns were on his mind tonight. He packed a variety of shiny objects and a few oddly shaped rocks that he considered to be "lucky" in some way or another. He wasn't completely sure what this journey would bring but he definitely wanted to be prepared. The meeting he was headed to would provide more details and he definitely didn't want to be late!

Walking towards his large roaring fireplace, Jimbo casually stepped into it without giving it a second thought and disappeared without a trace! Within seconds, he found himself engulfed inside a much larger bonfire. Through the flames, he could see the outline of several other spirits gathered around him. He stepped out of the large bonfire and made his way towards the gathering to take his place in the circle. He was incredibly grateful for portals and the time it saved him when trying to get anywhere on time!

The small circle of spirits were dressed in long gray robes with hoods that covered their faces. It was a dark night and very few stars could be seen through the dense forest trees surrounding them. Of course, spirits didn't actually need fire to stay warm or even clothes for that matter. No, this was a very special fire that would be used for teleportation into the World of Mortals or the Mortal Realm as it was called. Normally, a portal's destination could not easily be changed but this was no ordinary portal either. No, this particular portal was known as the "Fires of Avalon." Its protector had temporarily designated it as a gathering place for all the spirits who had been invited to the meeting. It was important to be on time because the portal's destination would soon change to a place soon to be announced. To miss a deadline in the Immortal Realm was to miss your entire mode of transportation completely! "Thank goodness I made it on time," Jimbo thought to himself.

The meeting was about to begin and the excitement in the air was so thick, it almost felt tangible! A white haired elderly gentleman stood in front of the small group and began to address them in a loud and mystical voice. "Gather closer please! I don't want to speak to loudly. There are many listening ears in this forest as you well know." The circle broke formation and the spirits gathered in front of the elderly gentleman. He continued speaking. "As you are fully aware, the Reaper has gotten out of control! He has gone on a killing rampage in the World of Mortals. I'm not exactly sure why this is happening but he must be stopped before more people end up dying before their time in mortality has reached its end!" The small group of spirits around him all raised a hand in the air and shouted; "stop the Reaper," in complete unison!

The elderly gentleman seemed happy they were all on the same page. "There are a few things I need to tell you before embarking upon this quest. We all know the Reaper's power was given to him by his superior Lord Hammond. Unfortunately, Lord Hammond is nowhere to be found at the moment and thus we have no direct way of contacting either him or the Reaper. That being said, we have gathered here tonight to go searching for both of them. We all know this to be a journey of the utmost secrecy and it should be treated as such!"

Something in the air blew up into Jimbo's nose and he couldn't help but let out a highly audible sneeze! "Sorry everyone," he said apologetically. "But since everyone is already staring at me, what are we supposed to do when one of us finds the Reaper?" The elderly man resumed his composure, "great question Jimbo! Hopefully the Reaper will listen to reason; but if not, one of you may need to capture and bring him back here until he decides to cooperate with us. The much easier option would be to get him fired! Remember, being a Reaper is simply a job and there are rules that even he must follow. We all know that the Reaper position was originally validated by the High Lord Zeus himself! It was originally intended to stop wicked people from causing too much harm and chaos within the Mortal Realm. Please listen carefully while I read to you the Reaper Rules that were carefully documented and set forth by Zeus himself." William unrolled a long brown scroll in front of his captive audience. "The Reaper Rules are as follows:"

1.   A Reaper may release **WICKED** spirits from their bodies **BEFORE** their time has expired within the Mortal Realm.
2.   A Reaper should collect **WICKED** spirits to add to the Pool of Lost Souls for safe keeping.
3.   A Reaper may never collect souls to use for personal gain.
4.   A Reaper may never release **GOOD** spirits from their bodies before their mortal clocks have expired.
5.   A Reaper must never attempt to harm another immortal being.

"These five Reaper Rules are important to remember because any attempt to break them would result in the loss of his job," said William pointedly. "To summarize, I recommend that you first try having a civil conversation with the Reaper in an attempt to be reasonable with him. Remind him that he is supposed to be stopping wicked souls from taking over the Mortal Realm, not enabling them. If he won't listen to reason, it may be necessary to involve a bit of trickery and perhaps some daring actions on your part in an attempt to get him fired! Lastly, if reasonable conversation or trickery won't work, you will need to make an attempt to actually capture the Reaper! I will tell you more about how to do that in a minute but first let's talk about the easier options."

"In order to get the Reaper fired, you will need to convince Lord Hammond that he has violated the Reaper Rules at some point. This would require proof that he has actually captured the souls of the innocent. Unfortunately, the chances of finding the captured souls are slim to none. There are places the Reaper can go that none of us even have access to. This is why trickery must come into play during this process. It will involve jumping in front of the Reaper's scythe while he is attempting to kill a mortal. We all know the Reaper's scythe is capable of freeing a spirit from its mortal body. However, if you make it look like the Reaper was trying to harm you during the process...this is in direct violation of the Reaper Rule of attempting to harm an immortal being! I know it sounds dangerous but as of yet a Reaper has never harmed a spirit before. Does this mean it's impossible? Hopefully none of us will have to find out. "

Jimbo interjected again. "This is so strange. Jumping in front of a moving blade was not my first thought when coming on this quest! But since we are all immortal beings, it's not like we have to worry about dying again right?" A slight chuckle came from the group. Jimbo continued, "by the way, for those of you who are wondering, my name is Jimbo Jenkins the Third!" A grouchy voice from the back yelled out, "nobody was wondering Jimbo!" The elderly man leading the group smiled and said, "since I am the one who invited each of you here tonight, you all know that my name is William. However, since the relevance of this quest does not depend on you knowing each-other, we will forgo with the introductions. This can be done on your own personal time if you so desire."

William glanced at the group of spirits around him. "I don't want to bore you all with a long history lesson but we all know that each Reaper throughout history has dramatically changed for the worse. Originally, he was supposed to only collect the spirits of wicked mortals. The goal was to stop them from causing too much harm and chaos in the lives of the truly good people. However, throughout time, each new Reaper became increasingly more power hungry and began to kill off many of the good people instead of letting them die of natural causes."

William paused to let his words sink in before continuing. "Of course, we all know that death takes on a whole new meaning for a spirit who has left the mortal body. No one wants to end up in the Pool of Lost Souls no matter how wicked they've been. The Reaper used to be known as the "Soul Collector" because he would collect evil spirits and add them to the Pool of Lost Souls. It's what many mortals would call "Hell." As of late, he has been collecting many innocent souls long before their time in mortality has expired as well. We are not sure why this is happening. However, we do know that the Reaper Rules clearly forbid it and it is causing serious problems for all realms involved. The Reaper must be stopped soon!" Someone in the audience shouted, "stop the Reaper!" The crowd followed suit by saying "stop the Reaper," in unison!

William nodded in agreement and continued. "Finding the Reaper's next victim may be a difficult task because we don't know when he will strike or who it will be. Also, keep in mind that he has a flexible portal that gives him the power to transport himself wherever he wishes within the Mortal or Immortal Realms. This gives us an unsporting chance at finding him as quickly as we need to. However, in order to give us a better chance at catching him, I have taken the liberty of acquiring about a dozen Stinging Scythes. Please bare in mind that these will only temporarily wound a mortal. This will draw the Reaper in to collect the wounded soul, thinking he or she will die. However, any wound you inflict with these weapons won't last long before it heals back up completely. Remember, the whole idea is simply to draw the Reaper in long enough to either talk with him, trick him or capture him. It doesn't matter which tactic you use so long as we stop the Reaper!"

William paused to look over at the barrel of Stinging Scythes not far off in the distance. "It is critical that you only use these Stinging Scythes on evil doers. Remember, the Reaper can only sense when WICKED people are dying. He won't show up for just ANY dying person in the Mortal Realm. On a related note, Lord Hammond would be able to help us more than we could on our own. Finding him first would be our best option. After all, he is supposed to be keeping tabs on the Reaper. Unfortunately, tracking him down is practically impossible but if you somehow figure out a way to do it, please don't hesitate to do so! Does anyone have any questions before we begin our journey?"

Jimbo raised his hand! "Um, how exactly would we capture the Reaper and what would we do with him if we did?" William looked up into the sky as if contemplating whether or not this was an actual possibility. "In the very unlikely event that you manage to get within touching distance of the Reaper, you will need to carefully detach the blade from your Stinging Scythe and physically touch him with the emerald crystal found inside of it. Allow me to demonstrate." William walked over to the large wooden barrel of Stinging Scythes and carefully grabbed one just beneath the blade. Lifting it out of the barrel, he began twisting the blade in a counter-clockwise direction. The blade twisted off the pole smoother than the lid on a pickle jar. Beneath the hollow blade stood a long pointy emerald crystal in the shape of a spear head. It sparkled by the light of the fire. "Touch this crystal against the Reaper and his very soul will be captured within your scythe. Of course, this is just a temporary hold until we can bring him before Lord Hammond," said William seriously.

William looked around at his awe struck audience. "I know many of you might be wondering, why even cover the crystal with the scythe blade? We do this because there are a variety of crystals that hold a variety of powers and we don't want our opponent seeing which crystal we are using until we actually have to use it! For example, the emerald crystal you see in front of you is called the Serpentine Crystal. It has the ability to capture immortal spirits inside of it. These are extremely dangerous weapons and it took quite an effort just to gain access to them! Each Stinging Scythe is equipped with a Serpentine Crystal inside of it. Please use them with extreme caution! That being said, does everyone understand the procedure for capturing the Reaper," he asked his awe struck audience. One of the spirits replied with, "I had no idea the Reaper could even be captured like that." William smiled, "it's not news that is widely published here in the Immortal Realm that's for sure. Usually, it's mortals who worry about this sort of thing. However, we know that it is our duty as good immortal beings to keep this rampaging Reaper in check!" It must have sounded like a rallying cry because the group followed by chanting. "Keep the Reaper in check!" William was happy that everyone seemed to be on board with his plan of action. "I am now going to have my assistant Skyler pass out the Stinging Scythes to all of you. This will better equip you for your journey into Mortal Realm."

Skyler was a skinny young man, about 21 years old with short blond hair and a narrow jaw line. He quickly moved over to a giant wooden barrel, removed a hand full of Stinging

Scythes and began dispersing them to each spirit in the group. There were only 12 people in the small group so it didn't take long to pass them out. Everyone began fondling their individual scythe with the utmost delicacy. The oblong curved blade attached to the end of each long metal pole was nothing to mess with! The slightest touch could easily cut through even a spirit's hand. Of course, it would never do any permanent damage. A spiritual body constantly regenerated in a way that caused him or her to live forever. At least, their history had not proven anything to the contrary so that is what they believed to be true. Also, no one within the Immortal Realm had ever seen another spirit die so it was simply a belief among them that all spirits lived forever!

Jimbo began to balance the blunt end of his scythe on the tip of his pointer finger. It was much lighter than he had anticipated. Being able to balance such a long object so well on just his pointer finger was incredibly intriguing for him! He glanced to the right and noticed another young man dressed in a long gray colored robe similar to his own. He was twirling his scythe the way a marching band leader would twirl a baton. Jimbo looked at him seriously. "It's a good thing we're already dead or I'd probably worry about you cutting yourself with that thing!" The young man chuckled a bit. "Yea, in my mortal life, I probably would have worried about such things as well. My name is Rooster by the way." Jimbo slammed his own Stinging Scythe into the dirt. "I bet you're an early riser," he said jokingly. Rooster laughed a little, well I'm usually up at the crack of dawn, similar to a rooster I suppose. That's basically what my family started calling me ever since...."

Before Rooster could finish his sentence, the ground beneath them began to shake! William shouted; "the Giants have found us! Everyone, into the portal quickly! We don't have much time!" One by one, the little group of 12 began to jump into the Fires of Avalon, meant for teleportation into the World of Mortals.

After all 12 had vanished from sight, William grabbed one of the charcoaled colored logs at the base of the fire. The log immediately began to grow in length and shrink in width until it transformed itself into a long black walking staff. The Fires of Avalon shot upwards in a long stream of fire until it dropped back downwards through the top of his walking staff. The once blazing Fires of Avalon was now trapped inside his long black staff; he turned to face the two heavyset giants standing behind him. "I don't want any trouble fellers. Please leave me alone."

The giants looked at each-other and then back at him. They were about 10 feet tall and were packed with large amounts of muscle all over their bodies. This was very apparent due to the minimum amount of clothing they wore. They were bare chested and only wore deer skin pants for covering. (Many had suspected the deer skin pants to have been stolen from the Underworld but no one really knew for sure.) They also carried giant wooden clubs held inside large metal sheaths strapped to their backs! One of the giants quickly unsheathed his heavy looking club. "We have strict orders to bring you in William. Lord Tidus has heard of your plans to stop the Reaper and we can't let that happen."

A look of seriousness came over William's face. "I would enjoy visiting with Lord Tidus. However, we can do this one of two ways. Either you let me come with you of my own free will and choice or we start a battle that could last an eternity. It's up to you!" The giants glanced at each-other again. "Follow us then," they both commanded simultaneously. William chuckled, "walking is old fashioned boys! Both of you touch the handle of my staff and we'll be there in no time flat!" Both giants touched the handle. "Now, I want you both to think of the exact location of Lord Tidus right at this moment," William continued. "Are you both picturing his location in your minds?" Both giants nodded. "Excellent! I command the Flames of Avalon to reappear," said William confidently. Immediately the staff began to melt beneath their hands. The fluid like substance began to move in a circle around the three men as if it were alive! It quickly ignited into giant blue flames that surrounded their bodies. The flames continued growing taller and taller until even the giants had to look up at them. Each individual flame joined forces at the top and formed a complete enclosed circle around the three of them.

Both giants looked mesmerized by this sudden display of power! It was the first time either of them had seen such a thing. William watched their reactions carefully and smiled to himself. "Well boys, it's time to take that leap of faith through the flames! We've arrived already. I can tell you fellers aren't used to portal travel are you?" Both giants looked at each-other and one of them shook his head, "I don't think so. You go first." "Oh, don't be afraid," said William. "It's merely a portal that has taken us directly to Lord Tidus. Assuming that is where you were both thinking of, right?"

William didn't notice a third giant slip into the ring of fire behind him and without warning; a giant club smacked him over the head! William was out like a light! "Good work boys! I never could have opened this portal without you!" The third giant standing behind the fallen William was much more muscular, taller and dressed like a king! "Thank you Lord Tidus," said one of the giants gratefully. "This is why you are our wonderful and amazing leader, because you always come up with the best strategies that no one ever thinks about." "I do my best," Lord Tidus said casually. "Well come on, let's not waste any more time! Everyone touch the portal and focus on

Lord Hammond's location. We need to get to his place quickly!" All three giants put a hand inside the wall of flames that surrounded them and intensely focused on where they wanted to go. Each of them was thinking about Lord Hammond's location. If their thoughts had not been in unison, the portal wouldn't have gone anywhere.

The three giant's stomachs began to churn. They could definitely feel themselves being transported through space and time at an incredibly high rate of speed! They were not used to traveling by portal and would normally enjoy walking wherever they wanted to go. They all took a moment to catch their breath before stepping outside the portal and through the ring of fire. Lord Tidus grabbed William's arm and dragged him through the flames. Once they were all out of the fire circle, Lord Tidus reached his right hand into the wall of blue flames and commanded them to transform for him. Immediately, the fire began to transform itself back into the long wooden staff and into Lord Tidus's outstretched hand. He smiled to himself, knowing full well that he now possessed the Fires of Avalon and was about to speak with Lord Hammond concerning the Reaper. Indeed, his power was growing and a sudden air of invincibility washed over his entire being.

CHAPTER 2

HUNTING THE REAPER

Jimbo woke up. The first thing he saw upon opening his eyes were blue skies and a few white fluffy clouds floating directly above his head. He had no idea where the Flames of Avalon portal had transported him to. He sat up and began to feel some very stiff grass poking into the palms of his hands. He looked downwards only to discover that he was lying on top of a rather tall haystack! "Oh good," he thought to himself. "I'd much rather look for the Reaper out in the country than in a crowded and polluted city. I wonder where the other 11 people ended up going," he thought to himself curiously.

Jimbo had a million other questions racing through his mind when all of the sudden he smelled smoke. Something was on fire! He turned his head to the left and saw a young teenage boy in the distance. The boy was standing next to a tall haystack and was lighting it on fire! He seemed to be laughing about it for some reason. Jimbo noticed another tall haystack next to the boy that was already on fire! "What kind of trouble is this kid up to," he thought to himself. He was very aware that fires in the Mortal Realm were not used as portals. "The boy must have an incredibly devious motive for setting these haystacks on fire," he thought to himself. He rolled off the top of his haystack and onto the dirt below.

Jimbo stood up slowly when all of the sudden a hand covered his mouth from behind which easily muffled his attempts to scream out loud! Somebody jumped on his back and knocked him down to the ground. "Shhh...we don't want him to hear us!" Jimbo instantly recognized the unknown voice and the hand around his mouth let him go. It was Rooster! Rooster rolled his body off of him and tactfully remained in a crawling position behind the giant haystack in front of them. "Rooster, what the heck are you doing here," Jimbo asked excitedly! "The portal dropped me here too, same as you," said Rooster. "The important thing now is that we've found our evil doer and we shouldn't let him see us. Hurry and hide behind this haystack with me!" Rooster motioned for Jimbo to come closer to where he was so that the menacing teenager burning the haystacks wouldn't see them.

Jimbo laughed! "Are you kidding me Rooster? We are immortal spirits. He is a mortal being. He can't see or hear us at all! Rooster smacked the palm of his right hand against his forehead. "Of course, you're absolutely right Jimbo! I've been in the Spirit Realm far too long. I totally forgot that the mortals down here wouldn't be able to see or hear us. That being said, how are we supposed use our Stinging Scythes on them? They'll just go right through them!" Jimbo looked at him. "According to William, the Stinging Scythes are supposed to injure mortals long enough for the Reaper to show up. The Reaper will think the human is dying so he will appear to collect the injured soul. That's when one of us will need to jump in front of his scythe so that we can get him in trouble with Lord Hammond for attempting to harm an immortal. Does that make sense to you," Jimbo asked. Rooster nodded. "Yes it does. However, I don't like the idea of jumping in front of the Reaper's scythe. How do we know for sure that immortal beings can't die?" Jimbo laughed again. "Come on Rooster, we've already died once! We are immortal beings for crying out loud! We can't feel pain and we don't even need to eat or sleep for that matter." Rooster looked at him with concern. "True, but are you willing to take the risk based on something that could be a complete assumption on our part?" Jimbo laughed again. "I'm pretty sure we immortals can never be harmed….even by the Reaper. Don't worry Rooster, I'll be the one who jumps in front of his scary little blade if it'll make you feel better," Jimbo mocked. Rooster nodded. "Well that settles it. Let's go get that troublemaking kid shall we?!"

Jimbo and Rooster stood up from behind the large haystack they were hiding behind. They both realized just how silly it was for them to hide from mortal beings. After all, the troublemaking teenager running from haystack to haystack and lighting them on fire couldn't see them at all anyways. They also remembered that their Stinging Scythes would only work on evil doers and clearly this boy would have no good reason for setting haystacks on fire and laughing about it. Rooster and Jimbo pulled their Stinging Scythes from their harnesses attached to their backs for traveling and began moving forward towards the boy.

Rooster and Jimbo had to do some major running to catch up with the teenage troublemaker! He was a fast kid and definitely had a lot of energy. "Alright mister slash master; do your thing," said Rooster mockingly. Jimbo looked at him. "First, we need to plan this out just right because we don't want the Reaper knowing what we're up to until it's too late. I'll go in for the slash right before he sets that haystack on fire." Jimbo pointed towards the tall haystack next to them that the boy was now running towards. "Get ready to hide behind it and then we'll wait for the Reaper to show up." "Sounds like a plan," agreed Rooster.

They both stuck to the plan perfectly. Rooster slashed the kid across the neck with his Stinging Scythe right before he could set the nearby haystack on fire. The kid dropped to the ground like a sack of potatoes. Before hiding behind the haystack, Rooster noticed a glowing blue substance leaking from the cut on the kid's neck right where he had sliced him. It obviously wasn't blood but Rooster had never seen anything like it before. "Could it be spirit blood," he thought to himself. "No, spirits don't bleed. They can't die. We can't even feel pain," thought Rooster to himself as he ducked behind the haystack next to Jimbo. They both patiently waited for the Reaper to show up and claim the young man's soul. "Now remember Jimbo, you're the one who volunteered to jump in front of the Reaper's blade when he gets here!" "I know," said Jimbo quietly. "It really isn't a big deal. I keep telling you Rooster, we've already died once. We can't die again. We are immortal beings for crying out loud!" Rooster smiled. "Just keep telling yourself that buddy!"

The seconds waiting for the Reaper to show up felt like hours to Rooster since he was absolutely terrified of what might happen next. The air grew colder and the wind blew faster. Clouds covered the sun and without warning, a giant black and blue vortex appeared in front of the dying boy. The dark vortex hovered about a foot off the ground and swirled in a clockwise direction. A black hooded figure hovered out of it and slowly began descending towards the ground. The Reaper had arrived! Rooster caught a brief glimpse of him before ducking his head behind the large haystack standing between him and the Reaper. The Reaper was just as dark and menacing as he had imagined. He was covered in a long black robe that covered his entire body except for his hands and wrists which looked like they were made from pure bone. He also carried a long bladed scythe as if it were a part of his very being and never went anywhere without it.

Seeing the young boy lying against the haystack, the Reaper could tell what had caused his fatal injury. Looking at the blue substance seeping from the young man's neck, he knew immediately that another mortal had not done this to him. Nope, he had seen enough wounds in his life to consider himself an expert on them. This wound was obviously caused by a spiritual weapon. The Reaper knew that if the spirit was wounded bad enough it would cause injury to the mortal body as well. He looked around for the spirit who had wounded the young boy in front of him. He didn't see anyone so he assumed that whoever did it must have made their escape already.

The Reaper raised his long bladed scythe into the air and made a sideswipe towards the young man in an attempt to free his spirit from his dying body. However, before his scythe could hit its target, Jimbo jumped in front of it from behind the haystack to protect the dying boy. The Reaper's scythe slashed Jimbo right across the back! Immediately, the Reaper realized what he had done. "You fool," he yelled in his deep gravelly voice. "Do you realize what you've done?" Jimbo rolled his body off of the teenager he had landed on and faced the Reaper while lying on the ground. "Oh, I know exactly what I've done Reaper and you will pay dearly for what you've done here today!"

The Reaper laughed menacingly. "Oh, you think Lord Hammond will stop me do you? He is being taken care of even as we speak. You should concern yourself with more important matters. Even spirits can die young man!" This statement sent chills up Jimbo's spine! "No they can't Reaper! I've already died once. There's no way I'm going to die again," Jimbo yelled furiously! The Reaper laughed coldly. "Not yet you're not. But one day I will have the power to reap the spirits from the Immortal World. My powers grow stronger every day young man! Now, stand aside while I collect this troublemaker's soul!"

The Reaper twisted the blade off his scythe and quickly detached it from the pole beneath. Beneath the blade sat a pointy red gem stone. The blade must have been hollow in the center for the gem to be sitting under it like that. Holding the long curved blade in his left hand and the long pole in his right, the Reaper began speaking again. "Do you know what this bright red stone is called young man?" Jimbo suddenly remembered William giving the demonstration of how to pull the blade off of a scythe in order to use the crystal attached beneath it.

Jimbo's thoughts were interrupted…"it's called a Bloodstone," the Reaper continued. "Not just any ordinary Bloodstone; no. It was forged in the fires of Mount Olympus by Zeus himself. It was he who made my scythe and entrusted it to me for the reaping of souls."

"Um, I think you're leaving out a small detail Reaper!" Rooster stepped out from behind the large haystack he was hiding behind. "He gave it to you so you could collect the souls of the wicked! You seem to think that good and bad people are all the same lately. Also, you shouldn't be collecting innocent souls before their time is up in mortality. This needs to stop! Good people are dying in the Mortal Realm because of you Reaper!" The Reaper began hovering closer to Rooster. "Boy, spirits continue to live on in the Immortal Realm. It shouldn't matter to you how long they live in the Mortal Realm." Rooster interjected, "it matters because people still want to live long and joyful lives in mortality. It mattered to me when I was a mortal and I'm absolutely certain it matters to them," Rooster said passionately. (While Rooster continued arguing with the

Reaper, neither of them noticed Jimbo unscrewing the long curved blade from the end of his Stinging Scythe.)

The Reaper turned towards the dying teenager still lying against the large haystack. "You boys are distracting me from my duties," he said coldly. He pointed the end of his pointy red Bloodstone towards the dying teenager. A bright red stream of light flashed between the Bloodstone and the boy. The boy's spirit was about to be captured by the Reaper. Suddenly a burst of bright green light flashed from the glowing Serpentine Crystal attached to the end of Jimbo's outstretched metal pole. The green light slammed against the red light streaming from the Reaper's pointy Bloodstone. The Reaper looked at Jimbo with disgust. "Let go boy or you'll pay for this!" Jimbo continued holding his long metal pole in the direction of the dying teenager. "You let go Reaper! He's still young. He needs more time to live his life!" The Reaper held his ground. "He's an EVIL boy. He needs to be taken from this world," the Reaper said menacingly. Jimbo channeled his remaining energy into the long metal pole he was holding. "People can change Reaper. This young man can change!" Immediately, both streams of light transformed into a deep purple color and instantly vanished from sight! Before anything could be said, the dying teenager lying against the haystack in front of them began to breathe again. The cut on his neck had completely disappeared and his eyes slowly started to open. "See what you've done boy," the Reaper yelled angrily at Jimbo! "Hades will be furious when I tell him about this!"

Rooster began to scream at the Reaper. "What are you doing with all the souls you've been collecting Reaper? We know you've been collecting good souls along with the bad ones!" The Reaper screwed the long curved blade back onto the end of his scythe where it belonged. "It's none of your business boy," he said in his deep gravelly voice. "It is very much my business," Rooster exclaimed! "It is the entire Spirit World's business what you plan on doing with your collection of spirits! They belong in the Immortal Realm with us!" Rooster began twisting the blade off the end of his scythe. He was quick to pull the blade off the long metal pole and drop it to the ground!

The Reaper glared at the glowing Serpentine Crystal now being pointed directly at him. "Where did you get that," he asked with contempt. "I don't see how that's any of your business," retorted Rooster. "Where are the good souls you've collected Reaper? Tell us or pay the consequences," said Rooster threateningly! The Reaper laughed menacingly while swinging his scythe over his shoulder. "Don't challenge me boys! I've been through battles you couldn't even imagine!" Jimbo swung his scythe over his shoulder as well. "Yes, but those were mortal battles. We are spirits Reaper! You can't harm us!" The Reaper began to hover above the ground and slowly moved backwards towards the dark portal from which he had come. "When I have obtained the Krono Crystal, I will return for your souls young ones!" The Reaper turned his back on the young men in an attempt to reach his portal before they could catch him. Jimbo and Rooster began chasing after him with their scythes at the ready. Unfortunately, the Reaper made it back to the portal faster than they could catch up with him. He and the portal quickly vanished in a cloud of smoke!

Rooster looked at Jimbo. "Well, so much for Lord Hammond saving the day for us! I thought he would just appear after you jumped in front of the Reaper's scythe. Are you okay by the way?" Jimbo couldn't really look at his own backside to see if his wound had healed up or not. Being a spirit, he didn't feel any amount of pain from it. He turned so his back was facing Rooster. "See any cut marks back there?" Rooster checked him over quickly. "Nope, you're all good my friend." "See, I knew he wouldn't do any permanent damage," said Jimbo confidently. Rooster nodded, "thankfully that seems to be the case. I can't help but wonder what he was talking about when he mentioned the Krono Crystal though. Do you know what that was all about," he asked Jimbo curiously. "I'm really not sure," replied Jimbo. "Perhaps we should ask William if we ever get the chance to meet up with him again. I wonder what happened to him anyways."

CHAPTER 3

A PERFECTED MORTAL

The portal opened. William, Lord Tidus and his two giant servants had arrived at Lord's Hammond's place of residence…which happened to be just outside his bathroom door. The wall of fire encircling them diminished back into the walking staff Lord Tidus now carried. William was still out cold from the blow he had taken on the head. They heard a flush and knew that Lord Hammond was about to emerge into the open. Although the giants found their situation a bit comical, Lord Tidus was happy they hadn't been transported into the bathroom itself! It was almost as if the portal knew how to respect a person's privacy. "Thank goodness for that," he thought to himself.

Lord Hammond opened his bathroom door. A look of shock came over him to see this random group of strangers inside his home. He jumped back in fright. "Don't be startled Lord Hammond," said Lord Tidus quickly. "I'm sorry to barge in on you like this but it's an emergency my Lord." Lord Hammond quickly recognized the giant ruler, Lord Tidus. His large stature and kingly attire was hard to miss. After all, he was an incredibly muscular giant and he never went anywhere without his royal crown sitting atop his head as a continual reminder to other giants that he was indeed their ruler.

Lord Hammond was a human being who never actually died in mortality. He was one of the very few mortals who actually discovered and drank from the fountain of youth! Surprisingly, it was a total accident at the time. He was just a weary traveler desperately looking to quench his thirst when he stumbled upon a spring in the middle of the Amazon rainforest. Immediately after drinking from it, he quickly started having "delusions," as he called it. Many of his friends considered him to be absolutely crazy because he would see people that no one else saw and hear things that no one else heard. Eventually, it took an act of Zeus to set Lord Hammond straight on the whole matter. Since he was considered to be a perfected mortal, he had the ability to see, hear and talk to anybody in the Mortal and Immortal Realms. This made him the perfect choice to be the Reaper's boss! The Reaper had often made comments that "Lord Hammond would be a better Reaper than he simply because mortals would see him coming and that would give them a sporting chance at escaping their fate." Since the Reaper was a spirit, mortals were not able to see him coming and their fate was sealed whenever he decided their time had come.

Lord Hammond stood just under six feet tall and had a bit of a stocky build. Even though he didn't need to eat to survive, he still enjoyed it. However, that also meant he needed to use the restroom every now and then simply to eliminate all the unnecessary waste in his body as well. He had a well-trimmed brown beard and mustache and looked like he was in his mid-forties. Although, age really didn't matter in the Immortal Realm since no one had been known to die there anyways. Spirits simply looked whatever age they had looked their best at while in mortality. Apparently, Lord Hammond must have looked his best at the age of 45 because that's about how old he looked now.

Lord Hammond began speaking in his gruff sounding voice. "What is such an emergency that you can't use the doorbell Lord Tidus? Also, why is this man out like a light? What kind of trouble have you brought with you?" Lord Tidus began speaking again, "My Lord, once again, I'm sorry to trouble you but my business is regarding the Reaper. The man you see lying on the ground in front of you has organized a group of spirits to stop the Reaper from performing his duties in the Mortal Realm."

"Why in the world would he want to stop the Reaper," Lord Hammond asked curiously. "That is a great question my Lord," Lord Tidus replied. "The truth is that this man doesn't want any more spirits coming into the Immortal Realm. He thinks they are all much more evil than they used to be and so he would rather have them all trapped inside their mortal bodies rather than coming to live in the Immortal Realm with us." "Oh, that's a horrible thought," Lord Hammond replied. "Yes, we thought so to..." Lord Tidus continued to lie. "A group of my servants have so generously volunteered to stop this group of spirits before they stop the Reaper from doing his job. However, in order to stop them, we would need your Spirit Staffs. Would you mind if we borrowed a few of them? I hope that's not too much to ask?"

Lord Hammond thought for a second and then replied..."Lord Tidus, the Spirit Staffs were used anciently to capture evil spirits who walked inside the Mortal Realm unchecked. There were to many troublemaking spirits who needed to be removed from the Mortal Realm. This is why mortal possession happened so frequently back in those days. Once they were removed, all of the Spirit Staffs were given to me for safe keeping." Lord Tidus interrupted him, "with all due respect Lord Hammond, I am aware of the history behind the Spirit Staffs. I am also aware that they are able to capture any spirit whether they be good or evil. Thus, I can see the dangers of having the Spirits Staffs fall into the wrong hands. That being said, I give you my word that once me and my men have captured the 12 spirits who have gone in search of the Reaper, we will return every one of your Spirit Staffs without delay!"

Lord Hammond seemed impressed by the way Lord Tidus was negotiating for the Spirit Staffs. "I trust you Lord Tidus and obviously your people trust you as well. Just curious, how did you know there were 12 spirits going after the Reaper?" Lord Tidus replied, "I have spies who watched their secret meeting from a distance my Lord." Lord Hammond nodded. "I appreciate your honesty. Please follow me to my cellar and I will retrieve the Spirit Staffs for you." Lord Tidus nodded as well. "Of course." He turned towards the two giants standing next to him. "You two stay here and TAKE CARE OF William if he decides to wake up while we're gone." He made sure to emphasize the words "take care of," so they knew exactly what he meant. Lord Hammond looked at the two giant servants. "That's very thoughtful of you Lord Tidus. If you want to leave William in my care when you leave, I would be more than happy to take care of him." Lord Tidus scowled a little. "With all due respect Lord Hammond, we brought him here so he is our responsibility." Lord Hammond looked at poor William passed out on the floor in front of him. "I trust your men will take excellent care of him when he wakes up. Follow me Lord Tidus," he commanded.

The two men made their way into the living quarters where a large stone fireplace stood etched into the wall. Lord Hammond picked up the long metal fire poker leaning against the mantel and used it to push aside a large wooden log.

Behind the log sat a stone with a three pronged indentation. It was so small that most people would not have noticed it unless they were really looking closely. The three pronged indentation matched up perfectly with the tips of the three pronged metal poker. Lord Hammond inserted the prongs into the indentations and twisted once to the left and then twice to the right. Immediately, the entire fireplace began to lower itself into the ground. Gradually, a long spiraled staircase began to appear before them gradually descending downwards into the abyss.

Lord Tidus looked at Lord Hammond. "I am impressed good sir. You hide your cellar quite well!" Lord Hammond looked flattered. "I appreciate the compliment. I do what I can. After all, we can't trust everyone now can we?" Lord Tidus shook his head. "Indeed we cannot."

Before descending down the long spiraled staircase, Lord Hammond pointed towards the two torches mounted on both sides of the wall where the fireplace used to be. "Grab one of those my friend. You're going to need it down here." Lord Tidus grabbed one of the torches off the wall and Lord Hammond grabbed the other one mounted on the opposite side. "What shall we use to light them," Lord Tidus asked. Lord Hammond pointed towards a small black button on the side of the torch which he pressed in and slid upwards. Immediately flames erupted from the top of the torch and it began burning brightly. "Thankfully, technology has much improved these days," said Lord Hammond with a laugh. "In the Mortal Realm, kids are using what they call flashlights and cell phones for light these days. Apparently, they're like torches that take a while to burn out but they don't keep a person warm though." Lord Tidus looked intrigued, "sounds absolutely fascinating!"

With their torches lit, the two continued walking down the spiraled staircase. It was a long decent into the dark abyss below. However, Lord Hammond had a lot to talk about. He continued, "I have had the privilege of mingling in the Mortal Realm for quite some time now and believe me they are truly an inventive sort of people. They actually invented a box that has moving pictures on it! It's truly incredible! The humans are so mesmerized by it that they will sit in front of it for hours just staring at the blasted contraption!" "How intriguing," said Lord Tidus with amusement in his voice.

"I must say Lord Hammond, I don't think it's fair that you get the privilege of mingling among the mortals and I don't. Simply because you're a perfected mortal that can be seen and I'm nothing but a giant spirit." Lord Hammond chuckled a bit. "Oh Tidus, it's really not everything it's cracked up to be. Seriously, I can't even tell the mortals that I'm actually an immortal because they would just laugh at me and say I've gone insane! That's how they are in the Mortal Realm. They're skeptical of everything. I could be Zeus himself and they would tell me to prove it!" It was Tidus's turn to laugh. "I suppose you're right Lord Hammond. I remember being mortal myself and that wasn't enjoyable at all. There weren't many giants living at the time and smaller humans were trying to kill off the last of us. I'm really not sure if they succeeded because I passed away before I could find out."

Lord Hammond chimed in, "how did you pass away Lord Tidus?" "Oh, some arrogant little kid threw a rock at my head," replied Lord Tidus. "I'm sorry to hear that my friend," said Lord Hammond sympathetically. "Yea, he killed my father Goliath the same way too so I was out for revenge! Things didn't work out in my favor sadly." The two men continued walking down the twisted staircase in respectful silence. "Wow, someone sure must have had a heck of a time digging the pit for this cellar," said Lord Tidus trying to lighten the mood a little. Lord Hammond laughed. "Rumor has it that an old witch used to live here. Apparently, magic created everything down here including this incredibly long staircase!"

Lord Tidus chimed in again, "I'm not sure I really believe in magic. I mean, we know there are major differences between the Mortal and Immortal Realms and that spirits can do things that mortals can't do. However, magic is a bit of a stretch for my imagination Lord Hammond." Lord Hammond became a bit more serious. "Well, did you ever believe in ghosts when you were a mortal?" Lord Tidus shook his head. "No, I didn't even believe in an afterlife." Lord Hammond continued walking down the stairs. "See, just because we don't believe in something doesn't mean it doesn't exist. By the same token, our beliefs don't always shape our reality either. For example, I might believe that this staircase will take us straight into the Underworld but that doesn't make it true either."

The two men continued talking and walking down the long twisted staircase until they finally reached the bottom. In front of them stood a long narrow hallway lined with multiple doors on the right and left all made of metal. Thankfully, their torches still burned bright enough to see the pathway ahead.

"Now if I remember correctly, the Spirit Staffs should be located inside the fourth door on the right. I believe I marked the door last time I was down here," said Lord Hammond confidently. Both men began counting the number of doors they passed on the right. Sure enough, the fourth door had been marked with a picture of two crossed staffs. "X marks the spot," Lord Hammond said with a laugh. He twisted the dusty old door handle and pushed forward. Walking through the open door, the two men stepped into a rather small room. In the center of the room stood a tall wooden wardrobe with two golden handles held together by a lock and chain. Lord Hammond reached into his pocket and retrieved a little golden key. "Would you do the honor," he asked Lord Tidus. Lord Tidus nodded. "It would be a pleasure!" Accepting the key from Lord Hammond's outstretched hand, Lord Tidus quickly inserted it into the dusty old padlock and twisted. An audible click told them the old padlock had been successfully unlocked. Pulling the chain from between the handles, he dropped it and the padlock to the floor. Grabbing a handle with each hand, he began to pull the wardrobe doors open.

To their surprise nothing was inside except for an overly sized mirror attached to the back wall. There was also a tiny note stuck to the top of the mirror. Lord Hammond reached for it immediately. He began reading it out loud so Lord Tidus could easily hear him.

"I have borrowed your Spirit Staffs for the time being Lord Hammond. There are troublemakers in the Underworld that need to be dealt with!"

"Your Well Intentioned Servant,"

Hades

Lord Hammond smiled. "Hades is quite the character. He seems to get certain terms mixed up sometimes. Like the words "borrowing" and "stealing" seem to mean the same thing to him," he said with a laugh. Lord Tidus became very serious. "He didn't have a key to the wardrobe did he?" Lord Hammond shook his head. "No, that is exactly what puzzles me. I am the only one with a key so I really have no idea how he managed to steal the Spirit Staffs or even find his way down into this dark cellar for that matter. I mean, he is a powerful man but it's not like he had a direct portal going into the wardrobe did he? Even if he had a flexible portal that he could control at will, he would still need to know where the Spirit

Staffs were located before he could portal to them. As far as I know, I was the only one who knew where they were. This whole scenario is quite puzzling to me Lord Tidus!"

Lord Hammond slapped the palm of his right hand against his forehead. "How could I be so stupid! The large mirror at the back of the wardrobe has to be the portal that connected Hades into the wardrobe! I always wondered if that mirror had some sort of historical significance and now I am fairly certain of it!"

Lord Hammond walked towards where the large mirror was propped up against the back of the wardrobe. It almost looked like it belonged there as if it were a part of the wardrobe itself. "I wonder who put this here," he thought to himself. He could see his reflection in the mirror just like he could with any other mirror. Pausing for a second, he admired his charming figure. Even though he carried a few extra pounds, he was still proud of his full head of dark brown hair and his well-trimmed beard and mustache. Sure, his mustache curled upwards at the ends and almost gave him the appearance of a villain but he knew that was definitely not him.

Lord Tidus cleared his throat which seemed to break the trance that Lord Hammond had put himself into. Before getting carried away in his own reflection even further, Lord Hammond reached his right hand towards the glass. He knew that if this was indeed a portal as he had suspected, his hand would simply fall through to the other side of it. Sure enough, his hand fell right through the glass as if nothing had been there at all! Lord Tidus gasped as he watched Lord Hammond glance back at him for a brief second before continuing to step through the glass into the unknown. Lord Tidus was quick to follow his footsteps. He stepped through the mirror just as Lord Hammond had done. Thankfully, the mirror was large enough for even an eight foot giant to step through. Granted, he had to duck a bit to get through but that wasn't a problem for him.

Stepping through to the other side of the portal, Lord Hammond and Tidus found themselves inside what they thought was an incredibly large cave. This was unlike any cave they had ever seen before. The first thing they noticed was the massive smooth slab of rock they were walking on. It was the largest and smoothest dark slab of rock they had ever set foot on! It was as if the cave floor had been carved and smoothed out by a giant machine and it continued as far as the eye could see.

The second thing they noticed was an extremely large pool filled with glowing green slime right in the middle of the cavern! The pool looked to be over 10 feet in depth. Lord Tidus could tell it was much deeper than he was tall. They walked up next to it and looked down inside it. Both men were deeply disturbed by what they saw. Deep inside the green glowing slime, they found millions of tiny spirits all swimming around endlessly. Many of the spirits saw them looking into their pool and began banging on the outer wall as if it were a prison they couldn't escape from. They cried out for help but couldn't shout or bang on the pool wall for long because they had to continue swimming to keep themselves afloat. It looked like they were doomed to swim around the pool endlessly for all eternity! Both men could see how excruciating this punishment would be for the wicked spirits who ended up inside of it. They both felt extremely glad to not be a part of their torturous world.

"Aw yes, I see you boys have found the Pool of Lost Souls," said a cool baritone voice from behind them. Lord Hammond and Tidus jumped with fright. They were not expecting to see anyone in this dark and lonely place. They turned around to see a dark cloaked figure hovering effortlessly above the ground and slowly floating towards them. He was tall and slender with neatly combed white hair and a long pointy chin. His robes were black and his entire body was covered in blue flames! As he came closer, they both felt a chill run through their bodies as if the flames would freeze them instead of burn them.

Lord Hammond was the first to reply. "I hope you'll pardon our intrusion Hades but I got the note you left inside the wardrobe and..." Hades interrupted him, "and you wanted to come down here to the Underworld to get the Spirit Staffs back from me I imagine?" Lord Hammond nodded, "that is the general idea, yes. Although, I had no idea there was a portal leading straight to the Underworld right inside the wardrobe." Hades laughed. "Obviously, I don't tell you everything Lord Hammond but like I mentioned in the note, I am trying to rid this place of some very pesky future intruders." Lord Tidus jumped into the conversation, "future intruders? How do you know that's even going to happen?"

Hades looked at Lord Tidus thoughtfully, "I am Lord of the Underworld. I can see things before they happen down here Mr...." "Lord Tidus is the name," said Lord Tidus in an effort to introduce himself. "I am the Lord of the giants!" Hades smiled a very crooked kind of smile. "You'd be surprised how many giants have ended up here in the Underworld Lord Tidus. They were quite a brutal bunch at one time!" Lord Tidus nodded, "I don't make excuses for the faults of my people. They have their struggles just like everyone else I suppose."

Hades looked downwards towards the large glowing Pool of Lost Souls. "Well gentlemen, being Lord of the Underworld has its perks and one of them is being able to see the future of this place! Two spirits will soon appear in search of the Reaper. They will refuse to leave the Underworld until they find him. Of course, only ill-mannered guests would overstay their welcome. Thus, I feel it necessary to either extend their stay for an eternity or get them to leave as quickly as possible. After all, if they are so insistent on not leaving than why not make their stay permanent if you know what I mean?" Hades smirked a little at his own cleverness. Lord Hammond and Tidus looked at each-other with befuddlement.

Lord Hammond briefly considered fighting Hades for the Spirit Staffs but thought better of it considering the uneven balance of power they would have in their current location. Instead, he decided on a more peaceful solution. "I'll make you a deal Hades. We'll help you find these intruders if you promise to give us the Spirit Staffs in return." Hades smiled. He loved making deals with people! "Catch those pesky intruders and the staffs are all yours! My only request is that you return them back to me once you have caught each one of William's men who have gone in search of the Reaper. Are we agreed?" Lord Hammond didn't like the idea of returning something that Hades had stolen from him in the first place but he knew that his chances of winning a battle with him in the Underworld were slim to none. So he extended his hand to shake on their new found deal. Hades looked down at his outstretched hand. "Considering that I am a spirit and you are a perfected mortal, we both know that my hand would go right through yours Lord Hammond." It was Lord Hammond's turn to laugh. "You obviously haven't been around many perfected mortals Hades. If you had, you would know that I have the ability to touch the spiritual as well as the mortal. Turns out, the fountain of youth gave me many abilities...some of which, I am still discovering."

Hades reached his right hand out to shake Lord Hammond's. "It's a deal then...oh, and you're absolutely right. Perfected mortals are rare to come by no matter what realm you're visiting. Follow me you two. Let's go catch those pesky intruders! I will show you some of the main tunnels and caverns they could be hiding in. Better yet…" Hades waved his flaming right hand in front of them and an old brown parchment appeared in his hands. "Let me just show you," he continued. All three of them gazed at the old parchment labeled, "Map of the Underworld," at the top. Turns out, the Underworld was far bigger than Lords Hammond and Tidus had ever imagined.

Hades pointed to a spot on the map labeled "Pool of Lost Souls." "We are obviously right here," he said simply. "I want both of you to follow this tunnel right here up to Ferryman's River. Since you both don't really know your way around the Underworld, just follow this river up as far as it goes. If you start to hear screams of pain and anguish than you've gone to far. I don't want you accidently walking into the Cavern of Torture without me. Nope, that place needs a good introduction at the least." Lord Hammond pointed to a place on the map called "Cavern of Deals." "What goes on in this place," he asked curiously? Hades rolled the map back up before they could get a chance to see anything else on it. "It used to be a place where I'd make deals with lost souls in order for them to get a second chance at life. It was fun for a while but I quickly started losing hope in humanity when I'd see them back in the Underworld after their lives were over. I used to believe people could change and become better but after giving so many second chances to so many people who never made it into the Immortal Realm after death; it just makes me sick to think about. Anyways, let's stay focused! We're gonna search this place better than a miner looking for gold! I wish you men the best of luck catching those pesky intruders," said Hades sincerely. "We'll do our best," Lord Hammond replied confidently. All three of them split up to go in the direction Hades had directed. "I can't believe anyone has ever feared this man," Lord Tidus thought to himself. Hades seemed like a well-mannered salesman from his perspective.

CHAPTER 4

THE REAPER OF ANIMALS

Jimbo and Rooster had been traveling for days. Open farm land surrounded them for miles. If they had been mortal and actually needed to eat, they probably would have stopped to break open a nice juicy watermelon growing in the outlying fields. However, they were spirits and didn't need to eat, sleep or drink. Their only real problem was the time it took to get from one place to another. Walking wasn't the most exciting thing in the world and finding portals wasn't easy either.

They were hoping to find some of the other spirits who had come into the Mortal Realm with them. However, the Fires of Avalon must have scattered them to other locations throughout the world. They weren't exactly sure where the others had gone. Thinking back to when they had first entered the Mortal Realm, they had assumed they would be surrounded by a large number of mortals. Unfortunately, this was not the case. They needed a way to lure the Reaper in and not having mortals around made things much more difficult for them. So they continued walking from one farm to the next. They walked past fields, farm houses, barns and quite a number of farm animals. They also had the misfortune of not seeing a single farmer out in the fields or farmhouses during their travels.

As they were walking, Rooster began contemplating how his whole perspective on death had changed since becoming a spirit. He never used to look at death in terms of a spirit simply leaving its body. He stopped walking. "Wait a second," he shouted excitedly! Jimbo stopped walking, only too happy for an excuse to stop being bored out of his mind. "What," he asked. Rooster pointed to a nearby cow in one of the fields. "I've never really thought about this before but do you think the Reaper might show up for a dying animal? Jimbo put a hand on his chin and thought for a moment. "That's a good question Rooster. I've never really thought about it before either. I suppose we could try using our Stinging Scythes on an animal just to see if someone shows up to collect the poor beast's spirit," he suggested. Rooster thought it was a great idea. "Would you like to do the honors this time Rooster," Jimbo asked. Rooster never liked the idea of killing anything but he agreed because he knew that the Stinging Scythes wouldn't cause any permanent damage.

Jimbo and Rooster walked over to where the nearest cow was standing. The cow's head was bent over and munching on the green grass below it. Suddenly the cow looked up and stared at them directly. "Do you think it can sense our presence," Jimbo asked thoughtfully. "Of course not," said Rooster. "Although, sensing and seeing are two different things. All that staring is starting to creep me out Jimbo!"

They continued moving closer towards the cow and it continued staring eerily at them as if it were somehow aware of their presence. Rooster reached for his Stinging Scythe attached to his back and pulled it from its harness. Raising the long curved blade high above his head, he aimed for the cow's stomach and swung sideways at it. Hitting his target, a large cut in the cow's stomach quickly became visible and a bright blue liquid began seeping out. Although it was not a mortal wound, it could still be seen by the two spirits looking at it. They thought of it as spiritual blood that would eventually cause the cow to become physically sick if it did not heal up soon. Thankfully, they both knew it was just a temporary wound and would heal up soon.

Jimbo and Rooster looked at each-other. "Now we wait," said Rooster patiently. "Perhaps we should hide behind something just in case the Reaper shows up again," said Jimbo thoughtfully. Rooster agreed and pointed to a nearby haystack. Quickly jumping behind the large haystack, they waited for the Reaper to show up again.

It wasn't long before a portal opened up next to the dying cow. A skinny looking feller stepped out wearing a straw hat and overalls. He looked like a farmer and even had a farmer's tan line on one of his wrists. Even though he looked like a skinny energetic farmer, he also carried a long curved bladed scythe over his shoulder which showed he meant business. This was definitely not what the young men were expecting at all! Jimbo stepped out from behind the haystack where they were hiding. "Hi there sir. My name is Jimbo. Are you the Reaper of Animals by chance?" The skinny guy in overalls hovered himself down to the ground. "The name's Tex and yes sir, I am the Reaper of Animals," he said tipping his big straw hat with one hand. He had a bit of a twang in his voice mixed with a southern drawl.

"I just have to ask," said Jimbo, "why are the Reaper of Humans and the Reaper of Animals two separate jobs?" Tex laughed a hearty warm laugh that actually made Jimbo smile. "Isn't it obvious kido? Think about how many people there are in the world. Now think about how many animals there are in the world. Heck, if I didn't have the ability to slow down time, I couldn't even handle the number of animals dying on a daily basis! Why, without me their spirits would be trapped inside their dead bodies forever! Also, I keep telling Zeus that we need an entire army of Reapers to do the amount of work we do on a daily basis! Heck, we should have a Reaper of Fish, a Reaper of Birds, a Reaper of Squirrels...the list could go on for miles! That's how I'd run the show if I were him but nooooo....he seems to think we don't have hobbies or need time for anything else in our lives! Sorry kids, I'm rambling now but what was it you wanted again?"

Jimbo smiled for a second. "Just curious, do you ever talk to the Reaper of Humans?" Tex shook his head. "Naw, our paths don't cross very often my friend. It's not often that animals and people die right next to each-other. Last time that happened was..." He looked upwards as if trying to remember. "A barn fire back in 1492 located in Yugoslavia somewhere...a poor farmer rushed into a burning barn trying to save the only two chickens he owned. Unfortunately, none of them made it out alive so me and the other Reaper ended up showing up at the same time; me for the chickens and him for the farmer. He asked me how business was going and I told him about the nearby forest fire that had caused me to work overtime. He told me he was getting tired of his job and was hoping to find a way out of it somehow. I told him to go talk to Zeus about it but we both know how much good he actually does to help any of us. Not much, I'll tell ya that!"

Rooster jumped out from behind the haystack where he was hiding. "Do you happen to know what the Krono Crystal is," he asked hopefully. Tex looked at him, his eyes wide with horror. "Now why would you ask about such a thing young man?" Rooster looked back at him confidently. "I'm asking because the Reaper told us he'd come back for our souls once he finds it!" A look of complete fear came upon Tex's face. "Well, I'm glad you told me that young man. What is your name again?" "Rooster's the name," replied Rooster energetically. "You seem to know what I'm talking about Tex. Do you?" Tex nodded. "Every scythe carries a certain type of crystal inside of it. That's what gives them their unique powers. Us Reaper's carry Bloodstones in our scythes. This gives us the power to harvest spirits or set them free from their mortal bodies. The Krono Crystal would allow the carrier to completely destroy a spirit! I know it's hard to believe that a spirit can die but Reapers throughout the ages have often searched for this Krono Crystal in hopes of one day ruling the entire Immortal Realm with its power! It truly is a unique dangerous artifact that no one can seem to get their hands on."

Jimbo looked terrified. "I've already died once and bloody well don't want to die again! How do we stop the Reaper," he asked desperately. Tex looked at him pitifully. "Well, the first thing you need to do is get him to come to you. Unfortunately, you can't do that out here in the middle of farm country that's for sure." Rooster jumped into the conversation, "we honestly thought the Reaper of Humans was in charge of every dying creature on the planet. We had no idea there was a separate Reaper in charge of dying animals but now we do. Sorry there isn't an army of Reapers out here to help you Tex." Tex nodded gratefully. "This job keeps me on my toes that's for sure! Thankfully, the ability to slow down time really comes in handy."

Rooster looked at him curiously. "What exactly do you use to slow down time Tex?" Tex pulled a little golden pocket watch from the inside of his inner robe. It looked like a regular clock with 12 black numbers going around a white circle but in the very center sat a blank digital screen. Two tiny push buttons sat on outer edges of the gold colored pocket watch as well. Tex began to explain the contraption he was holding. "This is what us Reapers refer to as a Collectors Clock. Normally, if a person or animal is about to die and only has so much time left to live, the screen will light up with the number of seconds left before the person or animal will die. However, if they begin to recover, the number on the screen will begin to increase in number. Of course, you have to actually point the clock towards them for it to work. The two buttons on the side allow me to slow down time and then resume it as normal when needed. Unfortunately, I can't actually go back in time or even stop it. Although, it would be nice, that's for sure!" That's really interesting said Rooster. "Mind if I hold it for a bit?" Tex put the Collectors Clock back inside his pocket. "Sorry, this is really meant for Reapers only. I'm sure the Reaper of Humans has one as well. Anyways, I better be off kidos!"

Jimbo interjected. "Wait, before you go, could you possibly tell us a little more about the Krono Crystal?" Tex looked at Jimbo. "Rumor has it that Hades once got a hold of the Krono Crystal. After all, Zeus himself came all the way down to the Underworld once just to look for it. He couldn't find it. So if Zeus couldn't find it there, I'm not really sure where it would be." Jimbo looked at Tex curiously. "Perhaps Hades is just really good at hiding things in the Underworld. In fact, we wouldn't mind taking a look down there if you wouldn't mind letting us use your portal real quick," Jimbo asked hopefully. Rooster looked at Jimbo. "Are you insane? We can't just venture into the Underworld and think that everything will be okay Jimbo! Spirits have gone there and never returned!"

Tex could see that this debate was about to get heated between the two young men. "Look fellers, a thousand animals just died during our little conversation here and I've got to get back to work so let's make this quick. Do you or don't you need a lift to the Underworld? Keep in mind, I probably won't be coming back this way any time soon." Jimbo and Rooster looked at each-other. "Alright, said Rooster. I don't like the idea of possibly never returning but I'll go!" Jimbo slapped him on the back. "That's the spirit my friend! Don't worry, we're going to be fine!" Rooster laughed. "You're a little too optimistic sometimes Jimbo."

Tex started hovering towards his portal. "Alright fellers let's get a move on shall we?" Rooster looked at the cow he had sliced open with his Stinging Scythe. The cut had completely healed up and the cow was moving and grazing on the grass like it had been previously. Jimbo looked at Rooster. "William did say that these Stinging Scythes would only cause temporary damage, remember?" Rooster nodded. "I'm really glad too because I didn't take any pleasure in hurting that innocent beast." Tex heard that and said, "I'm happy to hear you say that Rooster. To many animals get killed unnecessarily in the world and it makes my job that much harder trying to get to every one of them all the time. I also have a lot to say about animal cruelty but we don't have time for that right now. Let's get a move on boys!"

Since Jimbo and Rooster had never been to the Underworld before, neither one of them could picture it in their minds. They had to rely on Tex to get them there since he had actually been there before. They all linked arms with each-other to ensure their connection while traveling. The rules of portal travel made it impossible to get to any new destination without first travelling with someone who had been there before. The young men were extremely grateful for Tex's help because they simply wouldn't have made it to the Underworld without him. Of course, they didn't want the flexible portal taking them to the wrong place either, so they cleared their minds while letting the portal transport them to the place Tex had in mind.

CHAPTER 5

STEALING THE POOL

Stepping through the flexible portal, they stepped onto a large flat slab of rock. It looked like they had been transported to the inside of a dark cave. About ten feet in front of them stood a large green glowing pool of liquid that sunk deep into the earth. A number of stone steps led into its slimy depths. There was also an unusual amount of light coming from their right side as well. The group looked to their right only to find…another portal!

Rooster was shocked to see this! "Be careful guys, if another portal is here that can only mean someone got here before us and they're still here!" Jimbo looked at him. "Maybe another explorer has come looking for the Reaper or even the Krono Crystal," he said cautiously. Tex looked at the two of them. "Fellers, I hate to tell you this but this really isn't my quest. I only offered to give you a lift here and I've really got to get back to work."

"You can't just leave us in the Underworld without a way back," said Rooster desperately. Tex pointed towards the other portal right next to them. "Take that one if you need a way out," he said simply. Rooster looked at him. "Oh yea, right! We don't even know where that leads Tex! For all we know, that could lead straight to a fire pit Hades uses to keep this place warm!" Tex laughed. "Tell ya what, I'll give it a try real quick and tell ya where it goes if it'll make ya'all feel better?" Jimbo and Rooster nodded in agreement. "We would be very grateful," said Jimbo, trying to hide the absolute fear in his voice.

"Aw, it's not as bad as it looks," said Tex. "Trust me, there are much worse places you could have ended up." He stepped through the other portal before either one of them could ask what other places could possibly be worse than the Underworld. Both men stared at each-other. "I wonder if Hades knows we've invaded his territory already," said Rooster fearfully. "I doubt it," said Jimbo. "Hey, let's go take a look at that huge glowing pool of green slime," he said energetically. The pool wasn't too far away from the portal Tex had left in so they would easily be able to see if he were to return soon.

They both found it odd to find stairs going down into the eerie green glowing pool. "Who would even want to step into this slime," Jimbo said with disgust. They continued walking around the outer edge of the glowing pool. Staring down into it, they could see millions of tiny spirits swimming around endlessly. "This must be the Pool of Lost Souls where all the wicked ones end up," Rooster exclaimed frantically! I've heard rumors but never actually seen it before," he said with wonder in his voice. Jimbo put a hand to his chin thoughtfully. "This makes me so happy I wasn't such a horrible person during my mortal life," he said gratefully. "I agree with you on that one buddy," said Rooster feeling relieved his fate hadn't ended up like the poor spirits below him swimming around endlessly.

Just then a flash of light bounced off the cavern walls. Jimbo noticed it and looked over to where Tex had previously gone through the portal. It looks like he had returned already. "That was quick," Jimbo thought to himself. Jimbo and Rooster ran over to where Tex was standing. "So, what's the news? Where did the portal go," Rooster asked hastily. Tex looked at them. "Well, it looks like the portal goes to the inside of a wooden wardrobe. Don't worry, the wardrobe is open and it isn't locked or anything. I ventured around for a bit and it looked like it was located at the bottom of a very deep cellar. I'm not sure whose house it was but I did see a long spiraled staircase going back up to the opening entrance. So, I think you boys will be alright. Just remember that once you go through that portal, you will be inside someone's cellar. So it would be best to get out of there as soon as possible."

"Can't you just stay with us Tex," Jimbo asked hopefully. "I wish I could fellers but remember I have a job to do. In fact, the few minutes we've been here, a tornado just wiped out a whole heard of cows in Oklahoma! I've got to go set their spirits free otherwise they'll be trapped inside their poor dead bodies forever!" Rooster looked grateful. "Thanks for the help Tex. We owe you one for sure. Also, if you ever feel like checking up on us sometime, please do so." Tex smiled and shook both of their hands. "It has been an honor getting to know you boys. I hope things turn out in your favor. Also, I think you're quite the lucky bunch! I didn't think there would be an open portal down here that you could use to escape from the Underworld so take advantage of it if you really need to."

Tex looked upwards for a second as if he were carefully contemplating what he was about to say next. "I'd feel bad if you boys got trapped down here forever. So, if Hades gives ya'll any trouble just tell him that Morpheus has what he wants but won't give it up unless you guys are allowed to leave the Underworld unharmed and without delay. Got it?" A look of curiosity came over Rooster's face. "Wait a second, who's

Morpheus," he asked curiously. Tex started hovering back towards his portal. "Sorry, I've really got to get going kid. Just say what I told you to say if you get into any trouble down here. Trust me, it could be the difference between freedom and staying down here forever!" That said, Tex stepped through his open portal and vanished completely. His portal disappeared with him as well. The two young men looked at the other open portal that was still there. A feeling of relief came over them just from knowing there was a way out of that dark place!

Jimbo looked over at Rooster. "I think our friend Tex knows more than he's telling us. I mean, who the heck is Morpheus and what does Hades want from him? This whole adventure is starting to get really twisted Rooster." Rooster looked over towards the green glowing pool of water. "I think Tex was just giving us that little piece of information to help get us out of trouble if we really needed to use it. So don't go mentioning it to anyone unless you really need to," said Rooster tactfully.

Jimbo and Rooster walked back over to the large glowing green pool of water and began walking around its edges again. Its mesmerizing glow seemed to put them under some sort of trance. Suddenly Jimbo snapped out of it and blurted out the phrase, "Rooster, I'm having a crazy idea! I don't know if it's that tiny pool of spirits that gave it to me but I'm going to try something." Jimbo slid his Stinging Scythe from its harness attached to his back and began twisting the long blade off the top of it. He took off the hollow blade and dropped it to the ground next to the pool. The long emerald Serpentine Crystal sat just beneath where the blade had been. Its green glow was similar to that of the Pool of Lost Souls.

Rooster was quickly catching on to what Jimbo was about to do. "Oh no Jimbo, don't do it. Please stop!" But it was too late. Jimbo had shoved his long metal pole into the glowing green water! The Serpentine Crystal attached to the end began to glow with great intensity and all of the tiny spirits swimming around it began to be sucked up into it like a vacuum! It wasn't long before every tiny spirit in the pool had been sucked right into the Serpentine Crystal!

"What the heck are you doing," Rooster cried out! "Don't you realize this is Hades domain?! If he finds out that you're stealing his pool of wicked spirits, he's going to hunt you down with a vengeance!" Jimbo looked at him intensely. "Don't you get it Rooster? We are going to need some sort of bargaining chip in case we get captured down here. Yes, I know. Tex gave us that little bit of info about Morpheus but we need a backup plan just in case that doesn't work." Rooster interjected, "you're insane Jimbo!" Jimbo smiled. "Think about it Rooster. Being Lord of the Underworld is a JOB just like being the Reaper is a JOB. If Zeus finds out that Hades has lost his pool of wicked spirits, guess who's going to be in major trouble?" It was Rooster's turn to smile. "Ohhh...I see where you're going with this Jimbo....but I still think you're insane!" Jimbo laughed. "Trust me; you'll thank me if we ever get captured by Hades down here. Come on; let's get out of here before someone catches us!"

They quickly began making their way towards the open portal that Tex had previously checked out for them. With just a few feet left to go, they heard a deep mystical voice coming from behind them. "Now, just where do you think you boys are going?" The crackly baritone voice sent chills up their spines. Hades himself was hovering towards them at an intensely fast pace and was not too far behind them. He must have just come from of an adjoining tunnel because he definitely wasn't there moments ago.

"Come on Jimbo! Let's get through that portal before he catches us," said Rooster hastily. Suddenly Jimbo experienced a burst of bravery that began coursing through his veins. "No Rooster. Let's talk to him. I don't believe he can hurt us. After all, we've already died once remember?" Rooster slapped the palm of his hand against his own forehead. "You're such an idiot Jimbo," he exclaimed. Jimbo turned to face his fear and found himself face to face with the Lord of the Underworld. Surprisingly, he thought he'd be able to feel the heat of the blue flames surrounding Hades but instead he felt colder! It was as if the blue flames were meant to freeze objects instead of burn them.

Hades put a firm hand on Jimbo's shoulder and began speaking as if he were talking to an eight year old boy. "Jimbo, you shouldn't be here son. This is my world you know and I don't take kindly to intruders." Jimbo shook with fear. "How do you know my name? Also, we are here to talk to you about the Reaper." Hades smiled creepily and began speaking again. "I am Lord of the Underworld Jimbo. Even the walls of this place speak to me. They tell me everything they have heard." A chill went up Jimbo's spine. "Well then, you probably already know that the Reaper is after the Krono Crystal and we are trying to find it before he does."

Hades let go of Jimbo's shoulder and moved to his side. "And just what makes you think the Krono Crystal would be down here? You must already know that Zeus himself ventured down here once looking for it and came out empty handed." Rooster felt the need to say something. "Yea well, one can never be too careful. We're going to search this entire place until we find it!" Hades frowned. "You are a brave young man Rooster. I'll give you that but you really have no idea the kind of traps that are down here. Seriously, you're going to need a tour guide to show you around my domain if you plan on searching the entire Underworld! I'll have my ferryman guide you around. I would show you around myself but I've got much more pressing matters to attend to at the moment."

A lump formed in Jimbo's throat, "the ferryman? You mean the one who helps transport evil spirits across Dead Man's Lake into the Underworld." Hades smiled. "He could use a break. He's been getting tired of that job for quite a while now but hey, that's the Underworld for ya...repetitive misery on a daily basis!" Hades looked down at Jimbo. "But it's actually a miserable place for me as well Jimbo. Sure, I used to enjoy torturing evil souls and adding to their misery but over time, even I started to realize just how miserable I was myself! I mean, let's face it....some jobs we do just because Zeus assigns them to us, not because we want to." Jimbo looked at him unsympathetically. "Am I supposed to be feeling bad for you right now Hades," he said sarcastically. Hades smiled, "no, not at all...empathy is a heavenly trait Jimbo. We don't need any of that down here," he said with a smirk. Suddenly Jimbo actually did feel bad for not feeling bad about Hade's situation. Then he became confused because it was as if Hades had planned that entire conversation as a teaching moment to make him feel worse! "What a sly devil," he thought to himself.

Rooster interjected, "well, let's meet this ferryman of yours shall we?" Hades turned around and began hovering towards the opposite end of the cavern where he had previously come from. "Just follow me boys." Without another word, Jimbo and Rooster began following Hades towards where he claimed the ferryman was located." The blue flames continually surrounding his aura provided enough light to see their way through the darkness. Rooster just had to ask, "Um, I can't help but wonder if those blue flames ever cause you to burn up inside Hades?" Hades looked at him briefly. "If you must know, Zeus is the one who cursed me with these eternal flames.

They continually burn the life and happiness out of my soul. He did it so I could relate to all of the miserable souls who end up here in the Underworld. Believe it or not, I feel worse than the majority of people who end up coming here!" Jimbo had to stop himself from feeling bad for Hades. He didn't want to feel bad for the Lord of the Underworld, not at all!

Hades continued to lead them through a dark tunnel, into a cavern and through another dark tunnel which opened up into a larger cavern with a river flowing through it. The river was glowing green just like the pool of spirits they had seen earlier. Stopping next to the river, Hades reached into his inner robe and produced two gold coins. He tossed a gold coin to Jimbo and one to Rooster. "This is where our paths separate young ones. You will use these to pay the ferryman when he arrives." Hades bent down and put his right hand into the river. The green glowing river began to change to a glowing blue color almost as if his power was transferring itself into it. "What are you doing," Jimbo asked curiously. "If you must know Jimbo, I'm summoning the ferryman," said Hades with a bit of agitation in his voice. Removing his hand from the water, it changed back into its normal green glowing color again.

Within minutes, a large wooden raft was seen floating down the river. Standing on top of it was a skeleton covered in a long black cloak. Jimbo jumped back upon seeing the completely dead skeleton gently paddling the wooden raft down the river. "Don't be worried Jimbo. He's just an enchanted pile of bones destined to ferry wicked souls across Dead Man's Lake, down Ferryman's River and into the Underworld. He won't do much more than that. He wouldn't talk to you even if you wanted him to and believe me...I've tried," said Hades with a hint of loneliness in his voice.

The cloaked skeleton gently paddled his way over to the rocky bank where they were standing. The ferryman held a bony hand out towards them. "I guess this is the part where we pay him," said Rooster thoughtfully. Hades nodded. "This river makes a giant loop around the center of the Underworld. At some point during your journey, my ferryman will take a detour towards the Mortal Realm to collect the wicked souls who have passed on. Feel free to get off at that juncture. You probably wouldn't want to get caught circling endlessly around the Underworld forever! Unless of course you take some sort of twisted pleasure in being here than by all means stay as long as you wish. We could always use a couple of decent spirits to keep us on the straight and narrow if you know what I mean." The young men shivered to think of staying in the Underworld any longer than they absolutely had to.

Jimbo and Rooster each paid the ferryman the gold coin Hades had given them and they set sail immediately. The skeleton continued to paddle the raft down the river. Once they were almost out of earshot, Hades shouted, "Oh, I probably should have mentioned that once you get off the raft, you'll need another gold coin to get back on again!" Rooster quickly became enflamed with rage! "That two timing no good piece of…." Jimbo interrupted him. "Whoa there cowboy, let's not lower our standards just because Hades tricked us. I know we were going to search around the Underworld for the Reaper and Hades just sent us packing but we didn't leave empty handed my friend." Jimbo pointed his thumb backwards at the long scythe still strapped to his back. "Remember, we still got the you know what…." His voice trailed off as his head and eyes motioned towards the ferryman as if trying to tell Rooster that he was probably listening in on their conversation.

Rooster quickly caught on to what Jimbo was saying but decided to add his two cents anyways. "We need another gold coin to get back on this raft Jimbo! Once we're off...we're off! There's no coming back to search the Underworld!" Jimbo cut him short before he could say anything else. "Or, we could find the entrance to the you know what..." His voice trailed off again and he bent over to whisper in Rooster's ear. "We could find the entrance to the portal we found next to the Pool of Lost Souls. That would bring us back to the Underworld but let's not speak to loudly. I don't want this ferryman telling Hades what we're saying." Rooster shook his head. "I guess I shouldn't have expected any sort of help from Hades. He was obviously just trying to get rid of us as quickly as possible. That dirty snake!"

Jimbo agreed with him. "He definitely tricked us but I've got another plan." Rooster looked dumbfounded. "Okay Jimbo, what's your big plan? Just remember Mr. Bones here is still looking over our shoulders!" Jimbo frowned. "Hades said the skeleton only has one job and that he won't even speak to us remember?" Rooster laughed, "and you believe him I suppose? Wow, you really are gullible Jimbo! What if I told you I have a whole treasure chest filled with gold coins back at home. Would you believe me?" Jimbo smiled. "Really, well why didn't you bring them with you," he said playfully. Rooster palmed his own forehead, dumbfounded again.

Jimbo leaned over to whisper in Rooster's ear. "Think about it Rooster. How do you think all of the wicked spirits get on this raft before going to the Underworld?" Rooster thought about it for a second and whispered..."Holy Hades! They have to have a gold coin too! Where the heck do they get it from I wonder?" It was Jimbo's turn to link the pieces of the puzzle together for him. "Where else would they get a gold coin from Rooster? The Reaper of course! He has to give it to them so they can cross Dead Man's Lake into the Underworld. It all makes sense now. The Reaper would normally harvest the wicked souls with his Bloodstone and give a gold coin to the evil ones who aren't quite bad enough to be thrown into the Pool of Lost Souls. It's almost like there are varying degrees of evil and the Reaper has enough judgment to determine who should go to the Underworld and who should be added to the Pool of Lost Souls. I'm glad it's not my job to make that determination," said Jimbo thoughtfully.

A mental light clicked on for Rooster! "That is brilliant thinking Jimbo! If we want to come back here to the Underworld, we'll have to either take the gold coins from the Reaper or from someone who is about to cross over into the Underworld!" Jimbo slapped Rooster on the back. "Now you're getting it buddy!" Rooster was absolutely surprised he hadn't figured this out before now. "Your brilliance astounds me Jimbo! Way to go!" Jimbo smiled. "Well, I have been called a genius before," he said playfully.

They both looked up at the ferryman skeleton who had continued to paddle their raft down the river the entire time they had been whispering to each-other. They both hoped he hadn't heard what they were saying. But then again, he was simply a moving skeleton. "How much thinking or listening could he even do," they wondered.

They sat in silence as the ferryman continued to paddle them down the river from the back of the ferry where he stood. He stood in between two brightly lit lanterns that continually gave off enough light to see the entire ferry. The boys got the impression that those lanterns were probably lit by the same eternal flames that continually surrounded Hade's aura and would most likely never extinguish. Jimbo began wondering if the ferryman's paddling was even necessary because the current beneath them seemed to be moving them forward more than the paddling. There were many twists and turns in the river and the two young men couldn't help but stare at the glowing green water flowing beneath them. Its constant glow mesmerized them long enough to make them feel as if they were in a trance of some kind. It reminded Jimbo of the bright green Pool of Lost Souls they had seen when they first entered into the Underworld. He glanced backwards at the long protruding scythe he carried on his back and remembered how he had captured all the spirits from that large Pool of Lost Souls into his scythe. He was surprised that Hades hadn't caught him doing what he did. It kind of bothered him to think that maybe Hades did know but perhaps he let him get away with it only to cause more trouble for him later on. Hades was a sly devil and Jimbo got the feeling that this theft of his was going to come back to haunt him sometime in the near future.

The raft slowly moved around a river bend. Ahead, Rooster could see two people standing on the rocky shoreline waving at them. He wasn't sure who they were but he decided to call out to them. "Hello strangers! Who might you be," he yelled. A gruff sounding voice replied, "I am Lord Hammond and this is Lord Tidus. Please get off the raft so we can talk." Rooster replied, "it would cost us a gold coin each to get back on this ferry. There's no way we're getting off now." Lord Tidus responded with, "then we'll join you lads."

As the ferryman continued to paddle, Lord Tidus and Lord Hammond jumped on board to join them. Immediately, Lord Hammond grabbed Jimbo's hands and pulled them behind his back. Somehow he managed to tie his hands together using a small rope he pulled from inside the pocket of his dark robe. Lord Tidus did the same thing with Rooster. "I'm sorry to do this boys," said Lord Hammond, "but Hades sent us after some menacing intruders who stole his entire Pool of Lost Souls! You must be the thieves who stole them!" Lord Tidus grabbed Rooster's scythe and pulled it from the harness attached to his back. He twisted the blade off the top and pointed the long metal pole in a downwards direction. He began speaking to the Serpentine Crystal attached to the end of the pole. "Spirits be free! I release you now," he said in a deep commanding voice. Nothing happened. "Nope, nothing in this one," he said confidently.

Lord Hammond grabbed Jimbo's long bladed scythe from his back and copied what Lord Tidus had done. Only this time, a small amount of green glowing liquid came dribbling out. Lord Hammond quickly pointed the long metal pole upwards so as to not spill anything else out it. "Yep, looks like we caught the spirit thieves," he said with a tone of victory in his voice! Lord Hammond quickly reattached the curved metal blade to the end of Jimbo's scythe to keep the rest of the spirits from escaping.

Jimbo looked at Lord Hammond. "Look, I know we've got some explaining to do…." Lord Tidus interrupted him, "you've got a lot of explaining to do young man but you should save it for when we turn you over to Hades. I'm sure he can sort out a punishment for you!"

Rooster interjected. "The truth is, we've been trying to find you Lord Hammond. Well, we've been trying to find the Reaper but…you're the next best thing!" This statement caught Lord Hammond's attention since he was the one in charge of the Reaper. "Oh…" he said curiously, "and why would you be trying to find the Reaper?" Jimbo interrupted Rooster. "The Reaper has been on a killing rampage in the Mortal Realm and has been collecting a great number of innocent souls long before their time in mortality has expired! Please help us Lord Hammond before things gets worse!"

Lord Hammond looked at Lord Tidus. "You told me that William's group of spirits were out to capture the Reaper because there were to many evil spirits not fit to enter into the Immortal Realm! Now this young man is telling me that the Reaper has been needlessly killing innocent mortals before their time in mortality has expired! Who am I supposed to believe Lord Tidus?" Lord Tidus looked at Lord Hammond with a smirk. "Why would the Reaper go on a killing spree Lord Hammond? What motive would he have for that? It's a ridiculous story!"

Rooster looked at Lord Hammond. "Sure there are plenty of wicked spirits in the Mortal Realm but that's why the Underworld exists Lord Hammond. The wicked souls are collected by the Reaper and brought to the Pool of Lost Souls for safe keeping and the rest of the evil spirits are ferried into the Underworld by this guy!" He nodded his head towards the dead skeleton that was paddling their ferry down the river. Lord Hammond nodded in agreement. "Of course, I'm not sure why I forgot about that. There is only one way to find out the truth. I need to summon the Reaper to us. However, I can only do that if we find a portal."

Rooster began speaking again, "cut these ropes from our hands and I'll tell you exactly where to find a portal at." Lord Tidus interjected, "or we could turn these young ones over to Hades like we promised and claim the Spirit Staffs that we were promised in return." Lord Hammond frowned. "The only reason we are trying to obtain the Spirit Staffs is so we can track down William's group of Reaper hunters and stop them. However, if the Reaper is truly out of control like this young man is saying than it would be far more important to speak with the Reaper instead. Perhaps William is right about what he has been doing this whole time. This might change everything Lord Tidus!"

Lord Tidus's plan was falling apart but he didn't want to be labeled as the "guilty party" either. After all, "the King of the Giants shouldn't have a splotch on his good name," he thought to himself quietly. "Alright, let's see if the kid can tell us where a portal is," he said agitatedly. Lord Hammond pulled a small knife from beneath his sash and quickly cut the ropes that bound the two boy's wrists. "Alright kid, where can we find this portal you speak of?"

Rooster began massaging his wrists. "It can be found in the Mortal Realm. We know this ferry is going there now to help carry the wicked spirits into the Underworld. Once we get off there, I'll take you the rest of the way." Lord Hammond nodded in agreement. "I like the way you think lad. By the way, what is your name?" Rooster and Jimbo introduced themselves and the group continued their journey towards the Mortal Realm. The two young men couldn't help but notice that Lord Hammond and Lord Tidus never paid a single gold coin to get on the ferry. Neither of them mentioned this small detail to the ferryman since they felt like Lord Hammond was on their side now. Although, it felt good having a bit of leverage just in case they ever needed it!

CHAPTER 6

A DEAL WITH THE REAPER

Hades stared into the empty pool where his collection of wicked spirits had been not too long ago. He tried to keep calm but was boiling inside! He knew those pesky kids had stolen them right out from under his nose. On one hand, he was proud of them for doing it so smoothly. After all, encouraging bad behavior was part of his job description! On the other hand, he wasn't used to bad behavior happening to him! The Pool of Lost Souls had been doomed to swim around endlessly for all eternity and now they might have the opportunity to get a second chance if Jimbo were to set them free. The blue flames surrounding Hade's aura grew higher and much colder than usual. He was infuriated!

He hovered over to the open portal inside the dark cavern. He knew this particular portal would lead to the inside of the wardrobe where he had so cleverly stolen the Spirit Staffs away from Lord Hammond. "Well, if this isn't bad karma," he thought to himself. "I steal the Spirit Staffs from Lord Hammond and those punk kids steal my Pool of Lost Souls from me," he said angrily!

Hovering next to the open portal, Hades summoned forth a power from the depths of his blackened soul. His hands began glowing a bright red color as he touched the side of the swirling vortex. The inner vortex of the portal began glowing with the same bright red color as well. His authoritative voice began to fill the air. "Reaper, I summon you. Come to me now. I command it!"

Within seconds, a darkly cloaked figure began to emerge from the glowing red portal. He carried his long bladed scythe over his shoulder and his face was well covered by his pitch black hood. The Reaper hovered above the ground just like Hades was doing. They stared at each-other for a brief moment before Hades broke the silence. "Reaper, I want to make you a better deal than before. I know I offered you the Krono Crystal in exchange for a thousand innocent souls. However, the stakes have recently become much higher! Two young men just ran off with my Pool of Lost Souls! Bring them back to me along with all the other innocent spirits you have already collected and I will grant you the Krono Crystal. The two thieves are now heading towards the Mortal Realm on Dead Man's Ferry. They will soon arrive at the opening between the Mortal Realm and Dead Man's Lake. Get there before they do and bring them to me. You will then have your reward and believe me...the Krono Crystal is the only one of its kind as you well know!" The Reaper simply nodded in agreement and turned to enter the portal he had just come through. In an instant he was gone and Hades became much happier with his dire situation than before.

CHAPTER 7

DEAD MAN'S LAKE

Eventually, the river came to a juncture and the skeleton ferryman chose the path on the right to take them down. The group could only assume this was the path leading towards the Mortal Realm. It didn't take long before their assumptions were confirmed correct as the narrow river opened up into a rather large lake. They assumed this to be the dreaded Dead Man's Lake that legends had told about. Rumor was that a giant sea monster swam just below the surface just waiting to catch anyone who tried to jump off the raft in an attempt to escape their fate of going to the Underworld. However, no one wanted to confirm this rumor to be true!

Fog surrounded the entire lake and made it impossible for them to see past the shoreline from where they were located. Slowly sailing towards the shoreline, the fog cleared just enough to see a much larger group of spirits standing on a large wooden dock ahead. The group stood there, silently waiting to be ferried into the Underworld. It was as if they all knew the choices they had made in their mortal lives would eventually bring them to this point and they couldn't deny that it's exactly what they deserved.

Upon arriving at the large wooden dock, the group decided to get off the raft. They walked along the rocky shoreline for a bit before looking back at the raft. Almost as if by magic, the raft had grown much larger than it had been while they were on it! It was as if it were trying to accommodate the large number of spirits heading to the Underworld. Nobody in the group said it but they were all feeling extremely relieved to be out of that dreaded place. The thought of being stuck there for an eternity was a complete nightmare and they felt terrible for the ones who were headed there now.

Lord Hammond turned towards Rooster. "Alright, where is this portal you speak of lad?" Rooster pointed northward into the fog. "Follow me," he said confidently. The sun was setting and their light fading. There was enough light to see the tall grassy field in front of them. They continued trudging through the tall wet grass for about a mile before arriving at a large red barn. Apparently this is where Rooster had been taking them.

During their long walk towards the barn, Jimbo couldn't help but feel a bit concerned for Rooster. He was fully aware that Rooster had no idea where another portal would be located and that he was completely bluffing his way through their current situation. However, he didn't say anything to him because he didn't want Lord Hammond or Tidus to overhear their conversation and figure out what he was up to.

Upon arriving at the large red barn, Rooster motioned his left hand towards the closed doors. "After you," he said, looking at Lord Hammond. Lord Hammond was a good natured man but he was growing weary from traveling. "You better be right about that portal boy," he said as he reached for the black metal handle attached to the barn door. He pushed the handle downwards and then pulled it backwards towards himself. The barn door swung open easily. It was dark as night inside. "Everyone relax," said Lord Tidus. There is probably a lantern around here somewhere. He stepped inside and began feeling his way along the north wall of the barn. "Aw, there it is," he said with delight. He managed to find a lantern hanging from a small metal hook on the wall. "Good thing I always carry a tinder box with me for situations like this." Lord Tidus dug inside the pocket of his black robe and pulled out the tinder box he was searching for. Since Lord Hammond was the only one who could actually move mortal objects between the four of them, he sat the lantern on the ground and let Lord Tidus use his tinder box to help light it. Once the lantern had been lit, they began walking around the barn and found a few wooden stalls on the west side of the barn. Beautiful brown horses were inside the stalls and they began making much more noise now that their beauty rest had been disturbed by the four intruders.

"I still don't see a portal around here," said Lord Hammond with concern in his voice. Rooster looked around the barn. "Don't worry, a portal will appear soon enough" he said confidently. Rooster slid his long Stinging Scythe out of its harness from behind his back and raised it high above his head with both hands. "What are you doing," shouted Lord Tidus. Before another word could be said, Rooster had thrust his Stinging Scythe towards the brown horse standing in the stall next to him. He made a huge slice on the side of its belly and the horse cried out in pain right before toppling over to the ground. "What in heaven's name was that for," shouted Lord Hammond! "Don't worry, it's all part of my plan to get us a portal," replied Rooster.

Within seconds, a portal opened up just outside the horses stall. Tex stepped out and looked around. "Boy, I can't seem to get rid of you fellers," he said jokingly looking at Rooster and Jimbo. He then noticed Lord Hammond and Tidus. "Aw, pleasure to see you again Lord Hammond….and who might your friend be?" Lord Hammond smiled, "good to see you too Tex. It has been a while for sure. I think the last time I saw you was during the twister of 89! Boy that really ripped the place apart didn't it?" Tex smiled. "Don't remind me Lord Hammond. That mess took forever to sort out!" Lord Hammond began to laugh a little. "Funny, I'm starting to see what Rooster's plan was all along." He looked over at Rooster. "You're smarter than you look kid!" Rooster smiled. "Aw it ain't nothin' really." Tex looked confused. "Um, I'm not really sure what's going on here. I just came for this injured horse."

Lord Hammond didn't need Rooster to explain why he had summoned Tex. He was a fast thinker as well. "Hey Tex, I know you've got a job to do so I'll make this quick. I need to use your portal to summon the Reaper of Humans. Do you mind?" Tex got a curious look on his face. "Why, what's going on Lord Hammond?" Lord Hammond crossed his arms. "Well, to make a long story short...the Reaper has been collecting innocent souls before their time has expired in the Mortal Realm and we think he is looking for the Krono Crystal as well! I need to speak with him immediately because we both know the kind of trouble this is going to bring for everyone in the Mortal and Immortal Realms if he isn't stopped soon!"

Tex tipped his cowboy hat with one hand. "Oh boy, I don't even want to think about how many problems this could cause! By all means, use my portal Lord Hammond." Lord Hammond walked over to the giant spinning portal and touched the top of it with his left hand. He also began chanting. "Reaper, I summon thee! Come forth for your master!" Immediately a dark cloaked figure began to emerge from the black spinning vortex. The Reaper looked as dark and cold as ever. Lord Hammond turned to face him. "Reaper, speak to your master. Is it true that you have been collecting the souls of the innocent before their time in mortality has expired?" The Reaper began to speak in his deep mystical voice. "Hades offered me the Krono Crystal in exchange for a thousand innocent souls," he said simply. Jimbo and Rooster looked at each-other in shock and even Tex couldn't help but have a look of disappointment on his face. Lord Hammond continued speaking authoritatively. "Go back to Hades and tell him you will recover his Pool of Lost Souls in exchange for the Krono Crystal. Then return to me with his reply." The Reaper clasped his bony hands together and bowed to his master. Lord Hammond glared into the Reaper's glowing red eyes from beneath his hood. "Just remember, you are the one with a flexible portal. That means you will need to find us as we are not able to find you. Of course, I could always summon you again but let's hope I don't need to do that," he said agitatedly. The Reaper bowed again and began making his way back towards the dark vortex from which he had come. Almost instantly, the Reaper vanished through the portal just as quickly as he had appeared. Lord Hammond placed his left hand on top of Tex's portal to keep it from vanishing along with the Reaper. He didn't want Tex to be left without a portal.

Lord Hammond looked at Tex. "Thanks again for letting us borrow your portal for a bit." Tex tipped his hat. "Glad I could help." He looked over at the injured horse only to find that it had healed up already! "Well, would you look at that," said Tex astonishingly. Rooster looked at Tex. "I have to admit, I actually caused that injury just to get you here Tex. These Stinging Scythes were given to us by a guy named William to help us hunt down the Reaper of Humans." Lord Hammond turned towards Lord Tidus. "Speaking of William, whatever happened to him anyways?" Lord Tidus glanced off into the distance. "Oh, I'm sure my men are taking good care of him. Don't worry about that Lord Hammond," he said reassuringly.

Tex began walking towards his portal. "Well, I hate to run off on you fellers but animals are dying everywhere and someone's got to be there for them!" "Goodbye Tex," everyone said in unison as if it had been planned that way. Tex waved goodbye as he stepped through his portal. The last thing he said before vanishing was, "remember, ants are critters too." It was such an awkward thing to say that everyone couldn't help but laugh.

Jimbo was the first to speak after watching Tex disappear. "Thanks for offering to trade something I rightfully stole Lord Hammond," he said sarcastically. "I would have felt better about making the trade myself." Lord Hammond looked at him thoughtfully. "We were supposed to bring you back to Hades when we first found you sailing around on that raft. However, we figured it would be a better plan to go about things this way instead. We could have made things a lot worse for you Jimbo so please stop complaining!"

"Here's an idea," said Rooster out of the blue. "I'm just throwing this out there for contemplation but...maybe Lord Hammond and Tidus could go back to the Underworld and make the exchange with Hades instead of waiting around for the Reaper to come back with a response. I mean, who's to say that we can even trust him right?" Lord Hammond nodded, "that's an excellent point Rooster. Unfortunately, we still don't have a portal to get us there or anywhere else for that matter. Jimbo looked back at him, "well, it's just a thought, but how about we all sleep on it tonight and talk about various plans in the morning. Sure, I know we don't really need to sleep but I still get some joy out of it even though I'm immortal now." Surprisingly, the group agreed with Jimbo's request to discuss things in the morning so that they could all have time to form various plans as to how they could possibly proceed with their journey ahead. Even though physical exhaustion was never a possibility for them; emotional and psychological fatigue definitely occurred in and out of the Immortal Realm.

CHAPTER 8

WILLIAM THE PRISONER

William woke up desperately hoping it had all been a bad dream. He glanced downward only to find his hands and feet still shackled to the giant stone wall behind him. Glancing upwards he could see a glimmer of sunlight shimmering down from the barred window high above his head. The realization hit him again this morning. He was a prisoner to the giants who had captured and brought him there. He was already aware that the giants wanted the Reaper to succeed in his efforts for some reason. He wasn't sure why exactly but he knew that somehow they had gotten wind that he had gathered a group of spirits together to help stop the Reaper and the giants were trying to stop him!

Even though he was a spirit and could normally walk through mortal walls, these were spiritual shackles that bound him. Unfortunately, spirits could not pass through spirit walls in the same way that mortals could not pass through mortal walls. It also occurred to William that since he was immortal, he could be there for all eternity unless he found a way out soon!

William yanked his right arm away from the stone wall as hard as he possibly could. It was just as he thought, the wall wouldn't budge and his shackles were as solid as they felt! "It would take a miracle to get out of this," William said to himself. In the same moment, he heard someone coming down the stairs from behind the stone wall where he was sitting. Within seconds a giant prison guard was standing in front of him fiddling through a ring of metal keys. "This must be your lucky day," said the guard. "You have a visitor." William's imagination went wild. "Who could possibly know I'm here," he asked suspiciously. The guard eyed a particular metal key on the ring and began unlocking the shackles around William's wrists and ankles. "Turns out, Hades himself wants to see you," he said with an unmistakable "awe" in his voice. "Well, let's get a move on!" He put a hand on William's back and began pushing him towards the wide stone staircase. "Just be thankful you probably won't be our prisoner much longer," he said confidently. Happy to be free of his shackles, William followed the giant up the long stone staircase and into a large living room area. Looking around, he found himself in a luxurious living space filled with soft chairs, carpet and even a giant fireplace built into the wall. "It's hard to believe a dungeon is right below this," he thought to himself surprisingly.

The guard next to him stopped walking so William did the same. A large reclining chair facing away from them slowly began turning towards them. To William's shock and horror, his gaze fell upon Hades himself! As if the blue flames continually surrounding his aura weren't intimidating enough, his smile was much worse! "Well, well...if it isn't the great William," said Hades with a smile. "I've heard so much about you and now here we are...finally getting to meet each-other. Please have a seat." Hades gestured towards the open chair next to him. Looking up at the guard, he said gestured towards the doorway. "You may stand outside this room good sir and please remember to shut the door on your way out." The giant guard slammed the palm of his fist across his armor plated chest and bowed to Hades before exiting the room.

Hades looked back at William. "You and I have a few things to discuss William. First of all, those Stinging Scythes that you gave your little party to capture the Reaper with…we both know where those came from. Don't we?" Tension immediately began to build between the two men! William stood up from his chair and began shouting at Hades. "Yes, I took them from the Underworld but we both know they were only there because you stole them from Lord Hammond a long time ago!" Hades smiled again, "relax William. The only reason I'm upset is because one of your party members stole my Pool of Lost Souls using one of the Stinging Scythes that you so generously lent out to them. Do you understand what I'm saying William? It's one thing to take something that I rightfully stole but the Pool of Lost Souls has ALWAYS belonged to me William! I am going to make you pay dearly for this crime unless you can somehow make it up to me," said Hades furiously!

William sat back down in his chair and faced Hades. "I never told any of my party members to steal your Pool of Lost Souls Hades. That was never part of the plan. The plan was simply to stop the Reaper from killing more innocent mortals within the Mortal Realm. Why don't you find the real thieves and talk to them about it?" Hades rested his head against the back of the chair in an attempt to cool down a bit. "I found Lords Tidus and Hammond in the Underworld attempting to locate the Reaper. I would have kept them there for an extensive period of time for intruding into my private domain. However, after finding out that my Pool of Lost Souls had been stolen, I sent them after the real intruders. Instead of finding and capturing them like I told them to do, they ended up joining them and left the Underworld! William rested both hands over one of his knees. It was his turn to be skeptical. "Well, how do you know Lords Tidus or Hammond didn't steal your precious Pool of Lost Souls?"

The fire surrounding Hades quickly turned from blue to red and then back to blue again. It wasn't easy trying to hide his temper when the flames around him consistently betrayed his mood. Hades began to realize that he smiled a lot in attempt to calm the burning rage continually burning within himself. "I know because I searched them thoroughly before sending them to find the two brats who stole my precious Pool of Lost Souls! And before you bother asking me how I know there were TWO thieves...it's because I talked to my skeleton ferryman who ferried the four of them back into the Mortal Realm. I might add that Lords Tidus and Hammond never even paid the gold coins required for the ferry ride....which means they will both owe me a favor at some point in the future. No doubt all four of them are still searching for the Reaper and the Krono Crystal. Unfortunately for them, they will have to travel quite the distance on foot before finding a portal to take them anywhere. I assume they will find a way to summon the Reaper and since Lord Hammond is with them, the Reaper will no doubt follow whatever order that old phony requires of him! I would further assume that those thieves will want to trade what they've already stolen from me in exchange for the Krono Crystal...which I will not admit to having or not having at the moment."

Hades paused his monologue long enough to make sure William was still listening to him. William looked like he was absorbing every syllable in like a sponge. Hades continued speaking carefully. "Hypothetically speaking, if I did happen to know the location of the Krono Crystal, I probably wouldn't give it up so easily. This is where you fit into my plan William. If my calculations are correct, the Reaper will visit me very soon and tell me exactly what those lying little thieves want in exchange for the Pool of Lost Souls! So, instead of trading away the Krono Crystal...guess who's going to be traded instead," said Hades not bothering to hide the obviousness in his voice.

Before William could say anything, a dark portal appeared in the room between the two men. "Right on time," Hades exclaimed! Just like he predicted, the Reaper had appeared before their eyes. The dark cloaked figured stepped out of his swirling vortex and began whispering something into Hade's left ear. Hades nodded a few times and said, "I knew this would happen; Reaper. I want you to tell our thieving friends that I will be willing to exchange their friend William here for the Pool of Lost Souls that they have stolen from me. Unless they want to doom him to an eternity of imprisonment, I would highly suggest that they make the trade as soon as possible!" The Reaper nodded and bowed to Hades before returning back to the dark portal from which he had come.

After the Reaper stepped through his portal and just before it closed off into nothing, William took a giant leap forward from where he was sitting towards the portal. Diving head first into the closing portal, he somehow managed to get the first half of his body through the swirling vortex before it quickly sucked the rest of his body inwards and vanished into thin air!

Hades slapped his right hand over his forehead and screamed into the night air! "Noooo!! You stupid old man! Why couldn't you just do what you're told!"

CHAPTER 9

THE GREAT ESCAPE

Morning had arrived. Blue skies and bright sunshine blazed down on the little red barn where the group had slept the previous night. Rooster was the first to wake up. He stood up and stretched his arms. "I'm so glad we can sleep for pleasure and not because we need to," he said to himself casually. He looked around the barn at the rest of his party members. Lords Hammond, Tidus and Jimbo were all sleeping against haystacks piled in various places around the barn.

Rooster began to speak in a very loud voice. "I hate to wake everyone up but we should probably get a move on if we're going to find a portal to travel around faster." Jimbo began to stir into consciousness. "Now I know why they call you Rooster," he said with a smile. Rooster laughed. "Haven't heard that in a while," he replied.

Lords Hammond and Tidus began to stir from their sleep as well. Eventually, they were all up and gathered around the center of the barn. "I have to admit," said Lord Hammond, "even though we really don't need sleep to survive, something about it still feels really refreshing!" Lord Tidus nodded. "I agree. My thinking seems to be much clearer now that we've had some rest." Jimbo chimed in, "I had a brilliant idea last night that we should all take these horses to go in search of a portal to get us back into the Immortal Realm." Rooster looked a bit hurt. "I was literally going to say that very thing. Thanks for stealing my thunder there Jimbo!" Jimbo chuckled a bit and hit Rooster on the shoulder. "Great minds must think alike." "Apparently," agreed Rooster.

Lord Tidus was just about to tell the group that the horses didn't belong to them and he wasn't sure if they could carry a giant as big as himself anyways. But before he could express these particular concerns, a dark portal appeared next to the group in the center of the barn. They all recognized the dark swirling portal immediately. Lord Hammond stepped forward just as the Reaper stepped into the air and out of his portal. Surprisingly, another figure shot through the bottom of the portal in a head first position. The body shot a good ten feet through the air and landed on a nearby haystack. The group's attention turned away from the Reaper and towards the body who had just flown past them. The body struggled to get out of the hay and stood up to face them.

Jimbo was the first to recognize the old man. "William," he exclaimed with excitement! "What the heck are you doing here?" A deep growl came from the hooded Reaper. He was just as shocked to see William as the rest of them. He pointed a bony finger towards William. "You must come back with me. Hades wants you," he said commandingly. William shook his head. "Not on your life Reaper! You tell Hades that he will never take me prisoner again and I never want to see him again!"

Lord Hammond's attention turned back towards the Reaper. "Did you deliver our message to Hades," he asked curiously. The Reaper was still hovering in the air above the group. He nodded. "Hades wanted to trade William for the Pool of Lost Souls but now that…" William interrupted the Reaper. "I obviously escaped Reaper, so what do you plan on doing now," he asked mockingly! The Reaper continued speaking in his deep mystical voice. "I don't work for Hades." Lord Hammond nodded. "That's right Reaper. You work for me! Always remember that! That being said…I feel it my duty to remind you of your duties to humanity. First of all, I am completely ashamed that you ever had dealings with Hades to begin with. Second of all, if you are tired of doing your duties as Reaper, please tell me and I will find a replacement for you. Lastly, I feel the need to remind you of the Reaper Rules. There are only 5 of them so they shouldn't be that hard to remember and yes I always carry a list with me in case I ever need to refer back to them. I should have reminded you of these at our previous meeting but I'm going to do so now! Lord Hammond reached into his inner robe pocket and produced a small brown colored scroll which he unrolled. He cleared his throat as if he were about to make an announcement to the entire universe. The 5 Reaper Rules are as follows:

1. A Reaper may release WICKED spirits from their bodies BEFORE their time has expired within the Mortal Realm.
2. A Reaper should collect WICKED spirits to add to the Pool of Lost Souls for safe keeping.
3. A Reaper may never collect souls to use for personal gain.
4. A Reaper may never release GOOD spirits from their bodies before their mortal clocks have expired.
5. A Reaper must never attempt to harm another immortal being.

Lord Hammond rolled the scroll back up and placed it back inside his inner robe pocket. My sources tell me that you are currently in violation of rules 3, 4 and 5. Please explain yourself Reaper," said Lord Hammond commandingly.

The Reaper pointed towards Jimbo and Rooster. "They tricked me into thinking an evil person was dying and one of them jumped in front of my scythe before I could collect the little trouble maker's soul." Rooster interjected, "he was just a boy Reaper. He still had plenty of time to change his ways. One bad deed doesn't make a person completely evil." The Reaper continued speaking as if Rooster hadn't said anything. "Hades also offered me the Krono Crystal in exchange for a thousand innocent souls but I was going to set them free once the crystal was in my possession. Even Hades can't defend himself against Krono Crystal," the Reaper said truthfully. Also, my Collector's Clock has been stolen," he added as an afterthought, as if this bit of information didn't really matter.

Lord Hammond nodded. All the pieces of the puzzle suddenly came together in his mind. He looked up at the Reaper hovering above his head. "First of all, these boys summoned you in the only way they knew how. I don't blame them or you for what happened during that time. Second of all, I wish you would have just come to me to sort this whole thing out Reaper. There's no need to go around making shady deals with Hades for the Krono Crystal. I can tell you that he is Lord of the Underworld for a reason and would most likely not keep his end of the bargain no matter how many souls you collected for him. Last of all, you mention losing your Collector's Clock like it means nothing to you. This is how you keep track of how much time a mortal has left in the Mortal Realm. It is very important that we find your missing clock before you can continue doing your duties as Reaper. You say someone may have stolen it. Who do you think stole it?" The Reaper hung his hooded head as if ashamed of what had happened. "Hades took it. He claimed he was going to use it as collateral to make sure I kept my end of the bargain."

Lord Hammond looked at the Reaper very seriously. "Alright, I think it's high time I speak with Hades myself. Reaper, I'm going to use your portal to go speak with him. I want you to stay here and make sure your portal doesn't disappear when I leave. In the meantime, I need you to help transport my friends here back to the Immortal Realm. Then I want you to go around and gather up the other 10 spirits who originally came looking for you. You will need to have William here help you with that. He knows who they are and where they went." The Reaper was still floating in the air above the group and nodded in agreement.

Lord Hammond began walking towards the dark portal and then turned around to face Jimbo. "I almost forgot, I'm going to need your Stinging Scythe Jimbo since it has the Pool of Lost Souls inside of it. Jimbo carefully tossed his scythe towards him with the blade facing upwards. Lord Hammond snatched the long metal pole from the air and smiled at his own success. Suddenly he realized that Lord Tidus was nowhere to be seen. "Does anyone know where Lord Tidus is," he asked with concern. Rooster and Jimbo shook their heads. Lord Hammond shook his head as well. "If you guys could look for him I would greatly appreciate it. I need to get going. He waved at the rest of them and stepped through the dark portal. The Reaper touched the top of the portal with his bony left hand to prevent it from disappearing completely.

CHAPTER 10

A THOUSAND SOULS

William was the first to speak after seeing Lord Hammond disappear through the portal. "First of all, I just want to address the elephant in the room. I'm sure we all feel a little creped out with the Reaper standing right next to us. Second of all, it was the giants who locked me up! Not to point fingers or anything but we all know that Lord Tidus is Lord of the Giants. That would most likely explain his sudden disappearance. Last of all, before I made a desperate jump through the Reaper's portal, I was shocked to find out just how much Hades actually knew about our plan to find the Reaper. He had way more knowledge about our current situation than I ever suspected. This leads me to believe that he is only interested in our little group because it might end up involving the Krono Crystal which he eluded to during our previous conversation. I'm convinced that he knows exactly where it's located and is keeping it well hidden from everyone!"

That being said, William turned towards the dark cloaked Reaper floating in the air behind him. "What do you know Reaper? Does Hades know where the Krono Crystal is located?" The Reaper looked down at William. The air began to grow icy around them as if it had been triggered by William's question. "You are not my master old man," the Reaper said in his deep mystical voice. "I don't have to answer to you." William, Jimbo and Rooster quickly felt how powerless they truly were standing next to this dark mystical being.

William apologized. "I'm sorry Reaper. Of course you don't have to answer my questions if you don't want to. It's just that the Krono Crystal is one of the most powerful artifacts ever created and it's something that can and does concern everyone involved on this quest. No one is absolutely for certain but rumor has it that the Krono Crystal actually has the power to kill a spirit! Obviously, spirits in the Immortal Realm believe they won't ever die again and think the Krono Crystal is just a myth. However, we all know that Zeus himself actually descended into the Underworld to search for it. Now, why would he search for a useless artifact that didn't have any real power? No, I believe the legend to be completely true! Do you have any thoughts about it Reaper?"

The Reaper repeated to William what he had already told Lord Hammond. "Hades offered to trade me the Krono Crystal in exchange for a thousand innocent souls." William continued looking up at the Reaper. "Yes, I know that is what you told Lord Hammond. Did you take the deal," he asked curiously. The Reaper simply nodded as if he didn't feel the slightest bit of guilt for taking the deal at all. William continued, "well, obviously Lord Hammond just left to exchange the Pool of Lost Souls for the Krono Crystal but the real question is what are we going to do about those innocent souls you have already collected Reaper? That subject didn't even come up while Lord Hammond was here."

It was the Reaper's turn to speak. "The innocent souls belong to Hades now. I collected 732 of them." William's voice became very loud, "well, where the heck are they Reaper?!" A sudden wave of icy air came from the Reaper's being as if he was ready to turn them all to popsicles! William quickly realized how much rage was in his own voice and he apologized again for his sudden outburst of anger. The Reaper nodded as if to accept his apology and continued coldly. "Since you escaped from Hades, he will attempt to trade the innocent souls for the Pool of Lost Souls." William started to see the big picture of what was really happening. "It would seem that you and Hades knew more about this plan than any of us did. Thank you for the information Reaper. On that cheery note, let's go round up the remaining 10 souls I sent out to find you shall we?" The Reaper motioned his right bony hand towards the dark swirling portal as if to say, "after you!" He then rested his left bony hand on top of the portal to keep it from disappearing as William, Rooster and Jimbo all clasped onto each-other's shoulders before entering through the portal in a sideways single file line. The touching was necessary because only William knew where the other 10 people had gone to and this would keep them together during their teleportation through space and time. The Reaper was the last to enter through the portal before it finally vanished from sight.

CHAPTER 11

THE KRONO CRYSTAL

Hades found himself pacing back and forth along the hard flat stone surface of the Underworld. His plan had been completely torn apart the moment William had made his desperate dive into the Reaper's portal. Hades had already formed a new plan in his mind but was trying to think of something better as he really didn't want to give up the thing he so desperately wanted keep in his possession.

Hovering himself over to the giant empty pool where his lost souls had previously been; he stared into its empty depths and began contemplating possible silver linings to the black cloud of tragedy that had befallen him. "Well, at least this gives me the chance to look at my crystal again," he said to himself joyfully. Slowly descending the pool steps, he made his way to the center of it. On the stone floor below him was a large symbol of a star surrounded by three circles. He bent down and touched the center of the star with his right hand. The blue fire surrounding his body began channeling itself into it. Suddenly, the center of the star vanished as if it had never been there in the first place. Hades reached into the newly formed hole and pulled out a miniature sized treasure chest. Setting the chest on the ground, he flipped the two latches upwards to unlock the lid. Surprisingly, there wasn't a lock on it but Hades felt like its hiding place underneath the Pool of Lost Souls would most likely be the best place for it. After all, the last place anyone would want to look is under a giant pool filled with unsettled wicked spirits! However, since the pool was now empty, the perfect opportunity had presented itself to look into his little treasure chest without worrying about his Pool of Lost Souls trying to drag him down into its depths! Hades knew how miserable and frustrated the lost souls were and didn't want to imagine being caught in the same pool with them as well!

Reaching into the box, Hades gently lifted the one object that had been sought after for centuries! The Krono Crystal was in the shape of a spear head and its pointed tip looked just as dangerous as it felt. It was shaped perfectly to hide underneath a scythe's blade. Its deep orange color seemed too cheery for an object so deadly. It was originally created by Zeus's father, Kronos, as a weapon to destroy dangerous wicked spirits walking within the Mortal and Immortal Realms. Kronos had given this weapon to the first Reaper in existence in hopes that it would always be used as intended. Unfortunately, each succeeding Reaper began to grow more and more power hungry and wanted the power to control spirits within the Immortal Realm. This desire continued to grow until the Krono Crystal became highly sought after by the majority of Reaper's following the original.

Zeus never liked the idea of letting the Pool of Lost Souls suffer for an eternity no matter how horrible their crimes were in mortality. Since the Krono Crystal had the power to destroy a spirit, he ordered that it be turned over to Hades in hopes that he wouldn't make his Pool of Lost Souls suffer for all eternity. Eventually, Lord Hammond was able to reclaim the

Krono Crystal from the Reaper and reluctantly turned it over to Hades for safe keeping.

Hades felt comfortable living in the Underworld. He wasn't ready for a revolution against Zeus just yet. No, that would come later. But when the time was right, he would definitely want this powerful little artifact around to use at his whim and pleasure. In the meantime, he knew he could tempt and bribe future Reaper's and other spirits with the idea of possessing such power for themselves. He knew deep down that every spirit in existence really just wanted power and control for themselves. He also knew that everyone wasn't as lucky as he to have their own world to rule over. This brought him some satisfaction along with knowing that there were plenty of other souls out there far more miserable than himself.

His inner dialogue was coming to a close as he took a closer look at the Krono Crystal. It was glowing a bright orange color and could easily be spotted from long distances, especially in the dark. As a matter of fact, someone did spot it at that very moment. "Hades, I have come to make a deal with you," said a familiar sounding voice from across the room. Instantly, Hades recognized the voice belonging to Lord Hammond. Hades looked upwards from the deep empty pool he was standing in. "Sorry, I don't make deals with thieves," he said edgily.

Lord Hammond quickly made his way down the pool steps and reached the bottom faster than anticipated. "Hades, I will trade your precious Pool of Lost Souls in exchange for the Krono Crystal that you are clearly holding in your hands at this moment. What say you?" Hades was beginning to regret having pulled the crystal from its hiding place.

"Lord Hammond, you have to realize that the Pool of Lost Souls has always belonged to me from the beginning. You would simply be giving me something that you have already stolen and why would I want to give you anything in exchange for something that belongs to me in the first place?" Hades actually had a good point and Lord Hammond knew it. "You're absolutely right Hades. These lost souls do belong to you. As Lord of the Underworld, you are entitled to look after them. However, nobody in the Immortal Realm wants that Krono Crystal to fall into the wrong hands. We both know that Zeus himself came down here looking for it at one point in time and now I can see why he never found it." Lord Hammond's attention shifted to the small hole in the pool floor below where Hades was standing.

Hades laughed menacingly. "You really think I'm going to just hand you this incredibly powerful weapon old man? You've got another thing coming!" Lord Hammond pulled the long scythe from the harness attached to his back and began to unscrew the sharp oblong blade from the metal pole it was attached to. The long Serpentine Crystal quickly became visible and protruded from the long metal pole like a spear. Its deep green glow was easy to spot in the dark. "Hades, your Pool of Lost Souls is inside this crystal. I would be happy to crack it open and refill your pool again. All I'm asking is that you give the Krono Crystal to me for safe keeping. Hades shook his head. "How do I know you won't go mad with power old man? This crystal has corrupted even the most innocent of spirits. You would be surprised how insane others have become just at the thought of getting their hands on it!"

Lord Hammond came up with a quick plan. "Alright Hades, you're right. The Pool of Lost Souls belongs to you so I'm going to give them all back to you." This seemed to take Hades by surprise. Lord Hammond twirled the long metal pole in his hands a few times before smashing the pointy Serpentine Crystal downwards onto the stone floor. Immediately a large group of lost souls began flowing out of the broken crystal and into the empty pool where Hades and Lord Hammond were standing. "You fool," Hades yelled at Lord Hammond! The vast amount of lost souls flowing from the broken crystal began to grab onto Hades and drag him down into the pool with them. Lord Hammond took this opportunity to carefully swing his long metal pole towards the Krono Crystal held in Hatie's left hand.

His aim was perfect! He managed to smack the crystal out of Hades left hand and high into the air above him. The Pool of Lost Souls continued to drag Hades downward with them as more of them continued to escape from the Serpentine Crystal that Lord Hammond had smashed apart in the center of the pool. It was as if the pool of wicked spirits knew who was responsible for them being there and they all wanted revenge! The Krono Crystal continued falling from the sky and finally smashed against the pool's stone floor. In a flash, every single spirit in the pool, including Hades, turned to ash!

Lord Hammond witnessed the event and became incredibly grateful that he was more than a spirit or he would have been completely obliterated as well! Now more than ever, he was happy to have found the Fountain of Youth while in mortality which made him a perfected mortal being! He looked upwards towards the heavens. "Praise be to the maker of that blessed fountain," he said reverently. He needed a moment to process what had just happened. He took a moment to sit down inside the ash filled pool. In an instant, Hades and his legion of lost souls had been completely obliterated right in front of him! His gaze fell upon the glowing Krono Crystal lying on the floor in front of him. Its power was beyond anything he had ever imagined! He stood up and walked over to pick it up along with the long metal pole he had used to carefully knock the crystal out of Hade's hand. Unscrewing the remains of the broken

Serpentine Crystal from his long metal pole, he dropped it to the ground and began attaching the bright orange Krono Crystal in its place. He was surprised at how easy it was to break open the Serpentine Crystal to release the lost souls. He supposed that the sheer number them combined with their intense desire to escape was enough to help break it open so easily! Unfortunately for them, it was their punishment to never experience happiness in the Immortal Realm or ever again for that matter. Although Lord Hammond felt sympathy for the lost souls, he also felt like many of them probably wanted to be put out of their misery anyways. After all, who in their right mind would want to spend an eternity swimming around a large pool filled with other wicked spirits? "Talk about eternal punishment," he thought to himself darkly.

Lord Hammond managed to find the sharp oblong blade he had previously cast away from his scythe. He screwed the hollow blade over the top of the bright orange Krono Crystal. "That should hide it well enough for now," he thought to himself. Before leaving the pool of ashes, Lord Hammond spotted two gold coins lying on the floor where Hades had once been standing. He picked them up and recognized them instantly. They were ferryman coins! He admitted to himself that he really didn't have an escape plan when he first used the Reaper's portal to get into the Underworld but after picking up these coins…he knew exactly how he was going to get out of the there! He also remembered that he and Lord Tidus never paid the ferryman last time they had boarded the ferry.

CHAPTER 12

FINDING THE OTHERS

William, Jimbo, Rooster and the Reaper had been portal hopping all over the Mortal Realm in order to round up the other 10 spirits who had originally come on the adventure in search of the Reaper as well. Each spirit seemed surprised to see them emerge from the portal with the Reaper himself! Despite the Reaper's natural cold and distant appearance, Jimbo and Rooster had to admit that it was actually really cool to travel with him. If anything, it gave them bragging rights that most spirits didn't have the pleasure of doing the same thing. Also, it was really cool telling everyone else that they had accomplished their mission successfully. It was almost like telling the other questers that if their entire adventure had been a competition they were definitely the winners! Sure, the others seemed happy for them but Jimbo and Rooster sensed a bit of resentment that they were the lucky ones who had found the Reaper instead of them. "It seems like we should get a trophy of some sort," said Rooster jokingly. "Oh, we only saved the entire Mortal Realm as they know it," Jimbo laughed. "I'll have to be sure to record our adventures in the book I'm writing," said Jimbo casually. "Oh, what are you going to call it,"

Rooster asked curiously. "I think I'll call it Hunting the Reaper," Jimbo replied. "That's a catchy title," said Rooster. "Just remember to add the part where I single handedly fought off an army of giants while eating a green apple with my other hand," Rooster said jokingly. Jimbo laughed again. "You're a funny one Rooster."

One by one, the group rounded up the remaining 10 adventurers and brought them back into the Immortal Realm through the Reaper's portal. From there each of the 10 were able to find his or her way back to their individual homes. They all seemed a little uncomfortable standing next to the Reaper as if he would turn on them at any moment. Bragging rights aside, Jimbo and Rooster were still not completely comfortable traveling with the Reaper. His very presence chilled the soul and it felt as if all happiness was slowly beginning to drain out of them simply by standing next to him.

After the remaining 10 questers were rounded up and taken back to the Immortal Realm, William looked up at the dark hooded Reaper. "I've got one more place I need to go Reaper," he said with a slight tone of fear in his voice. "When the giants captured me, they also managed to steal my staff containing the Flames of Avalon. I hate the thought of returning to that vile place but it needs to be done." Jimbo looked at Rooster and whispered, "wish he would have thought of that before we made all of those awkward trips with the Reaper. We could have just used the staff's portal to get around instead!" Rooster ribbed him in the side as if to say; "quiet Jimbo, you're speaking way to loud right now!" William must have heard Jimbo's little comment because of his quick response. "Yes, I know we could have retrieved the staff first and then used it to make our other journeys without the Reaper but let's be honest...having the Reaper's protection is truly beneficial." Jimbo nodded in agreement. "Yes it is and I'm grateful for it for sure!" He didn't want to part ways with the Reaper without him knowing how thankful he was for the protection that he silently provided simply by being in their presence. Rooster must have realized the same thing because he chimed in with, "yes, thank you for traveling with us Reaper. You've been a great help! Also, we'd much rather be traveling with you than looking for you that's for sure," Rooster said thoughtfully.

The Reaper looked at the little group silently. "I will take you all on one condition." William looked at the Reaper. "What condition would that be," he asked cautiously. "You must promise to leave me alone when this is all over." All three of them blurted out the words "we promise" almost in complete unison. "Good," said the Reaper. "I will hold you to that promise," he said seriously. Rooster replied before he could even think about what he was saying. "If it makes you feel any better Reaper, we're only traveling with you because none of us have a flexible portal we can use to get around in at the moment. No offence but once this journey is through, I hope we don't have to see each-other again for a very long time." "I'm glad we agree on that," the Reaper said coldly.

One thing Jimbo and Rooster had quickly realized about the Reaper was that he only spoke when it was absolutely necessary. His social distancing combined with his dark and mysterious figure was only part of the reason they didn't feel comfortable around him. Even though they were grateful for his protection while portal hopping around the Mortal Realm, the thought of parting ways soon became the light at the end of the tunnel for them.

Looking into the dark swirling vortex, William clasped onto Jimbo's shoulder who then clasped onto Rooster's shoulder. Touching each-other was necessary because William was the only one who knew exactly where they were going and the other two didn't want to get lost in the vortex. William was the first to enter the portal followed by the other two. The Reaper had to always remember to put one of his bony hands on top of the portal while they did this to keep it from disappearing on him. After all, it was his portal and he didn't want it going anywhere without him! It didn't take long for the small group and the portal to vanish into thin air.

CHAPTER 13

THE VOICE OF MORPHEUS

Lord Hammond was slowly making his way through the Underworld in an attempt to locate Ferryman's River. With darkness all around him, he would normally have tried to find something to light his way. However, ever since Hades and the other Lost Souls had been destroyed, his entire body had been engulfed in blue flames similar to what Hades had before dying. He also felt a greater sense of inner strength and power. He thought perhaps the Krono Crystal might be lending him its power but it was just a guess.

The continually burning flames surrounding his body lit his way through the dark tunnels and passageways throughout the Underworld. The whole place looked like a giant cave. He was grateful not to be mortal at that moment simply because of all the other problems that could bring. Lost in a cave, a mere mortal would experience hunger, thirst and the extreme fear of possibly being eaten by a ravenous beast lying in wait. As a spirit, his only real worries were how to light his way through the dark, getting out of the Underworld and finding a portal to get to where he needed to go next. Considering it was the

Underworld, he might have a few other problems to worry about but he didn't want to think about that at the moment.

Lord Hammond could hear the sound of a river running nearby. A large rock wall seemed to be between him and the sound of the moving water. He didn't see any way around it. It was too tall to scale and too long to walk around. Suddenly he heard a deep and powerful voice inside his head say, "you are Lord of the Underworld now. Command the wall to move and it will move!" Lord Hammond stepped back in shock! That was definitely not the sound of his own inner voice. "Who are you," he asked out loud. The deep inner voice inside his head replied, "I am your new power. I am here to guide you as Lord of the Underworld." Lord Hammond laughed. "I don't want to be Lord of the Underworld. That was Hades job." His inner voice replied again, "He who slays the Lord of the Underworld must take on the task himself. It is written in the heavens and is now your duty to do so!" Lord Hammond continued to stare at the rock wall in front of him. "Who are you," he asked cautiously. "You may call me Morpheus," said his inner voice. "I am here to help you accomplish your new tasks here in the Underworld."

Lord Hammond frowned, "new tasks? What do you mean?" Morpheus continued, "Oh, there are many tasks you must accomplish as Lord of the Underworld. The first thing you should know is that before Hades passed away, he confiscated the Reaper's Collector's Clock! He did this to reassure the Reaper that he would not be breaking Reaper Rule number four. Do you remember what Reaper Rule number four is Lord Hammond?" Lord Hammond still wasn't used to the voice speaking inside his head. He kept looking around as if waiting for someone to jump out of a secret hiding spot and tell him this was all just a big joke. Despite his skepticism, he continued to reply to it. "Reaper Rule number four clearly states that "A Reaper may never release GOOD spirits from their bodies before their mortal clocks have expired." "Well done," said Morpheus agreeably. "The key phrase here is MORTAL CLOCKS. The only way the Reaper can tell if a person's mortal clock has expired is by using his Collector's Clock to find out. However, with the clock out of the way, it made it that much easier to collect innocent spirits without actually breaking the Reaper Rules. See what I'm saying Lord Hammond?" Lord Hammond nodded. "I understand. Where did Hades hide the Collector's Clock before he died Morpheus?" The voice inside his head continued speaking. "He hid it in a place far worse than this. He hid it in the place where spirits go to escape the Underworld." Lord Hammond palmed his forehead in frustration. "Quit playing games with me Morpheus! Where is this place you speak of?" A brief moment of silence followed his question. "I would be happy to tell you more Lord Hammond but I sense that your friends in the Immortal Realm desperately need your help at the moment. You should go to them quickly!"

Lord Hammond looked around at his surroundings. "How do I get there Morpheus? I was going to take the ferry into the Mortal Realm. Is there a portal down here in the Underworld that I'm not aware of?" He still wasn't used to speaking with the voice inside his head. "Now that you're Lord of the Underworld, your scythe may summon your flexible portal to you. Simply point the blade where you want it to appear and tap the long metal pole on the ground three times." Lord Hammond turned away from the large stone wall in front of him and pointed the curved blade of his scythe in the direction of where he wanted his flexible portal to appear. Tapping the long metal pole three times on the stony gravel below him, his flexible portal appeared just like Morpheus had predicted.

Since he knew where he was going, the portal knew exactly where to take him. Before stepping through the vortex he heard Morpheus say, "I should probably tell you that I can only speak to you from the Underworld Master Hammond. My powers of communication don't reach beyond this place unfortunately." Lord Hammond took one last look around. "You've been a great help Morpheus. Thank you and I suspect we'll speak again soon." With that said, Lord Hammond stepped through the open portal and vanished completely! He found it odd that Morpheus could only communicate with him inside the Underworld and yet somehow knew that his friends were in trouble outside of the Underworld. He made a mental note to ask him about that when he returned.

CHAPTER 14

FIGHTING THE GIANTS

The Reaper's portal finally opened up into the giant dungeon where William had recently been kept not too long ago. This is where they appeared because it was the closest place he could think of to where his staff might be located. The group began searching thoroughly for it. With the guards out of sight, it gave them a chance to search uninterrupted. Strangely, the Reaper did not search with them. He simply hovered in the air next to his portal as if waiting for the other three to finish their business. Rooster looked over at him. "Why aren't you helping Reaper?" Another burst of icy air was instantly felt by the group. "Sorry if I offended you," said Rooster apologetically. The last thing he wanted was for the Reaper to turn around and leave them without a portal to get out of that horrible place! The Reaper's cold mystical voice started speaking and since that didn't happen often the group quickly began to pay attention! "I do not care about your plans," he said darkly. "I am only here because Lord Hammond has ordered me to take you around in my portal. He did not order me to help you in any other way so don't expect it. I should leave you all here now and be done with you!" The entire group shouted, "NO," in complete unison! The giant guards must have heard them because one of them began shouting from the stone staircase above. "Who goes there? Who's down there?"

Heavy footsteps pounded their way down the staircase behind the stone wall where William had previously been shackled at one point in time. Those shackles looked too familiar to William and he definitely did not want to end up there again! He turned towards the Reaper, "please help us Reaper! I beg you! I will give you anything!" The Reaper looked down out William from where he was hovering in the air above him. "Find my Collector's Clock and I'll help you," he said promisingly. William nodded, "it's a deal Reaper!"

The giants had reached the bottom of the stairs and turned the corner around the stone wall to see the group standing in front of them. They halted their stride only to stare up at the dark luminous figure hovering above them. The Reaper began to draw his scythe from its long tubular sheath attached to his back. Holding the sharp bladed scythe in front of him, the giant guards stepped back in fear. They knew the power of the Reaper and what he could do to them. One of the guards made an attempt at bravery. "There's five of us Reaper and one of you. Don't think these little pipsqueaks would be a match for us. I should also remind you that we're spirits. We can't die!"

Just then, anther portal appeared in the room adjacent to the Reaper. Lord Hammond stepped out holding his long metal scythe in front of him as well. His scythe and body were covered in scorching blue flames! Surprisingly, the flames didn't seem to burn him at all. He began to hover in the air next to the Reaper. William seemed surprised to see Lord Hammond hover in such a way. The only people he knew who could do such a thing were the Reaper, Hades and Zeus himself.

The giants took a step back upon seeing Lord Hammond. Clearly there was more power in the room than they wanted to deal with at the moment. Lord Hammond began to speak authoritatively. "Bring Lord Tidus to us. I must speak with him immediately!" The leader of the guards could sense that they were overpowered. However, he and his men were ready to go down with a fight if needed. The guard leader pointed towards William. "What do you want with this old man," he asked furiously. William took this moment to interject a critical piece of information. "My staff has been stolen and we've come back to find it!" That was all the information Lord Hammond needed to start making commands, "yes captain, return William's staff to him immediately and then fetch me your leader Lord Tidus! It is critical that we speak as soon as possible." Another wave of desperate courage washed over the guard leader. "Look, I don't take orders from you! I only take orders from Lord Tidus and he wanted us to capture William here. Unfortunately, he somehow managed to escape from us. Thankfully, he's back again and this time we'll keep him here!" The guard leader reached out to grab William across the neck with his arm. William slammed his elbow hard into the giant's stomach behind him. The giant fell back from the force of the blow as his grip on William slipped away. The rest of the guards took this as a signal to move in closer on the intruders.

All five guards carried sharp pointed spears and began moving towards them. Jimbo and Rooster pulled their scythes from their harnesses to defend themselves against their attackers. Unfortunately for William, he was not armed at all. He began to back away towards Lord Hammond and the

Reaper for protection. It wasn't long before heavy metallic clanks were heard from spear hitting scythe and vice versa.

Even though nobody in the Immortal Realm had ever died before, battles had still been fought. The object was not to kill each-other because both sides knew that could never actually happen. The object was to let out all of the emotional pain, pride and frustration that was built up inside the individual. The reason battles could last for an eternity was simply because pride, frustration and a lack of self-justice could last for an eternity. The ideas of fairness and power were constantly being questioned in the Immortal Realm and could never be completely agreed upon.

Lord Hammond and the Reaper watched for a minute while the giant guards, Jimbo and Rooster continued to stab and slice at each-other. For them, it was much like watching children on a playground. Simply because they knew that unlike the World of Mortals, no real damage could actually be done. However, they knew that it could end up being a battle that could last for an eternity if it wasn't stopped in the right way. Lord Hammond and the Reaper looked at each-other. Although words were never spoken between them, the Reaper knew his master well enough to know what he was going to do. He nodded in understanding of their unspoken conversation and lowered his scythe in a non-fighting stance.

Lord Hammond slowly began to unscrew the oblong shaped blade from his scythe. Throwing it forcefully against the stone floor below him, the sound of metal smashing against stone with such force was enough to stop the fighters in their tacks just long enough to get their attention. Everyone in the room halted their attacks just long enough to find the source of the disturbing sound. Looking upwards, they all saw Lord Hammond majestically hovering in the air above them and pointing his long metal pole towards them. At the end of the pole stood the bright orange Krono Crystal! A sense of complete and agonizing fear flooded over the giants! Only myths and legends could have prepared them for this moment. They all knew of the Krono Crystal but most of them didn't believe it actually existed until now!

Suddenly, the realization dawned on the giants that they could be completely obliterated from existence FOREVER! It was a weapon that could kill a spirit itself…which they were! The captain of the guards ordered his men to drop their weapons immediately. He looked up at Lord Hammond. "I am incredibly sorry for disobeying you my Lord. Me and my men will run and fetch Lord Tidus immediately! You have my word." Lord Hammond nodded. "Go quickly then! Don't make me get angry!" The leader and his men quickly began running up the stone steps to go in search of Lord Tidus.

Lord Hammond smiled and looked at the Reaper. "It's amazing what so much power can do to a person hu?" The Reaper nodded in agreement and hovered a few inches backwards away from the glowing Krono Crystal. Even he was afraid of it. "Don't worry boys. I'm not going to harm you with it," Lord Hammond said reassuringly. "The real question is should I keep it for myself or turn it over to Zeus? What do you guys think? Rooster looked at him. "It would definitely be tempting to keep it that's for sure. I mean, just think about how much power and respect you'd have in the Immortal Realm." "Yes, I've thought about that," said Lord Hammond considerately. "Even Zeus himself would have to obey my every bidding," he said deviously. "However, if I did decide to keep it, I probably couldn't keep it a secret since those giants have seen it already. No, I should probably turn it over to Zeus for safe keeping. Let's all take a little trip to Zeus's palace shall we," Lord Hammond said with a smile.

William spoke up quickly. "I hate to interrupt everything that is going on here Lord Hammond but we still haven't found my staff yet, remember?" Lord Hammond looked at William. "I'm sorry William; I've got more pressing matters on my mind. I'll tell you what; I'll leave my portal here with you so that you and the boys can look around for your staff and still have a way to get out of here when you're done. Sound good?" William agreed. "Hopefully the giants have left the building by now so we won't have to worry about them anymore." "Oh, I'm sure they have," said Lord Hammond reassuringly.

It was Jimbo's turn to ask a question. "I just have to ask Lord Hammond, how did you find a portal to get out of the Underworld? I'm asking because I know you left through the Reaper's portal to get into the Underworld but never took it back with you." Lord Hammond looked down at Jimbo. "That's a great question Jimbo. I thought I was going to have to take the ferry out of the Underworld but I recently discovered that a flexible portal now resides within my scythe! You can imagine how grateful and surprised I was to find that out!" Rooster patted Lord Hammond on the back, "lucky you! Very few people in the Immortal Realm have their own flexible portal for personal use! Wish I had one." Lord Hammond returned the pat on the back to Rooster. "Perhaps one day you will lad. Keep hoping."

William began speaking again. "Well, come on boys…let's go find my staff! I hope you don't mind helping me." "Not at all," said Jimbo reassuringly. "Let's search this place," said Rooster hopefully. The three of them began to make their way up the stone staircase to search for the staff. When they were out of sight, Lord Hammond turned towards the Reaper. "I appreciate all the help you've provided old friend. I know I am your boss but I also consider you a friend as well. We have enough history together that I feel confident saying such a thing. I also know your cold emotional disposition won't allow you to feel the impact of what I'm saying but perhaps you can process it on a logical level." It all made sense to the Reaper. "I understand," he said with a nod. "Good," said Lord Hammond. "Well, let's go see Zeus shall we? I hate to give up the Krono Crystal but I suppose it does belong to him. It will probably be the safest in his possession. Also, I've got a few questions I want to ask him while I'm there. Hopefully he'll have time to see us with the busy schedule he has got."

The Reaper and Lord Hammond both had open portals swirling next to them. Lord Hammond decided to keep his promise to William by leaving his portal there for him, Jimbo and Rooster to use if they needed it. Lord Hammond entered through the Reaper's portal. Both of them knew exactly where Zeus's palace was located so they didn't feel the need to touch each-other in any way before entering through the portal. Lord Hammond was the first to step through the dark swirling vortex before completely disappearing from site. Like usual, the Reaper kept his bony hand on top of the swirling vortex to keep it from disappearing on him. Before entering the vortex himself, The Reaper pulled a long staff from beneath his long dark cloak and pointed it towards the other portal from which Lord Hammond had arrived. Within seconds, the other portal shriveled up into a stream of light which flew directly into the long black staff he was now holding. The staff glowed with power! The Flames of Avalon now belonged to the Reaper! The Reaper quickly hid the staff beneath his cloak again. "Good thing I'm tall enough to fit the staff underneath my cloak," he thought to himself. He quickly entered the portal and followed his master to the Palace of Zeus.

CHAPTER 15

THE PALACE OF ZEUS

Unfortunately, a spirit could simply not portal into the Palace of Zeus. All visiting portals were designated to appear outside the palace inside the portal parking lot. The majority of portals in the parking lot were fixed portals, meaning they were designated to be there and would not disappear just because someone travelled through them. Fixed portals would take a person from point A to point B and never disappear. Whereas, flexible portals would take the traveler wherever he or she wanted to go and would close off on one end after doing so. Unfortunately, the majority of spirits in the Immortal Realm did not own their own flexible portals. Only the highly privileged spirits owned them and rarely let others use them.

So when a flexible portal suddenly appeared in the palace parking lot, passersby couldn't help but stare at the privileged new arrivals, especially when the Reaper himself was one of them! The Reaper was rarely seen in the Immortal Realm simply because his job mainly kept him inside the Mortal Realm most of the time. It was hard to miss the feeling of complete aloofness and coldness the Reaper carried while passing by him. Although, with Lord Hammond by his side; the coldness carried a feeling of power and confidence with it as well.

The two men quickly made their way to the palace entrance. Two guards stood in front of the tall golden gate which stood in front of the large wooden door behind it. Since the guards were not worried about being harmed, they didn't worry about wearing armor either. Instead, they wore long white robes with golden sashes and carried tall golden tridents.

One of the guards stepped towards the two men. "I'm sorry gentlemen but Zeus is not seeing anyone today. His schedule is booked solid for another month but I would be glad to get you on the schedule if you'd like?" Lord Hammond laughed. "Do you see the Reaper standing next to me young man?" The young man looked at the Reaper and began to feel an icy chill in the air almost immediately. The guard shivered. "Well, I'm sure it must be an urgent matter since the Reaper is with you. Let me see what I can do to get you both in right away. Please wait here for a moment. I'll be right back."

He whispered something to the other young guard before walking towards the golden gate. Looking up at the guard standing on top of the wall above the golden gate, he shouted "open the gate Phil! I need to speak with Zeus for a moment." Seeing that it was a fellow guard who gave the order, Phil and another guard began twisting what looked like a very large ship helm at the top of the gate. The giant gate began raising upwards and the young guard walked through. Upon reaching the large wooden door, the guard reached into his inner white robe pocket and produced a silver key. Twisting the silver key into the nearby lock, he then pulled a long metal lever downwards next to it. This must have unlocked the large wooden door in front of him because it began swinging inwards.

Lord Hammond and the Reaper looked at each other. They each knew what the other was thinking. They needed to make a run for it! They quickly hovered themselves beneath the tall golden gate and through the giant open door before either of the guards could close it again. One of the guards saw what they were doing and began shouting to the guards standing above the gate; "intruder alert, intruder alert!" The guards standing on the wall above the gate quickly closed it but it was too late. The intruders had slid right past them!

It didn't take long before Lord Hammond and the Reaper were quickly surrounded by guards, all holding sharp pointed tridents. It was mandatory for them to be taken to Zeus for questioning. (But of course, this was all part of Lord Hammond's plan to have a meeting with Zeus without having to wait an extra month just to get on his schedule.)

The guards marched the two intruders down a long hallway and stopped in front of two tall intricately crafted metal doors which led into the Throne Room. Once inside, a deep and majestic voice called out to the guards. "Bring them in." The guards felt a little awkward escorting two men who could hover in the air above their heads. Clearly, the balance of power was not equal here and they were glad a fight had not broken out between them.

Zeus stood up from where he sat on his golden throne. His appearance was that of a wise old sage. He stood a little over six feet tall and wore a long white robe that only covered one of his shoulders. His other shoulder was completely bare and one could tell that he was a muscular man simply by looking at his exposed arms. His hair was long, white and neatly parted on the side. His beard and mustache were neatly trimmed and he carried a long golden staff inlaid with a variety of brightly colored jewels that sparkled when the light hit them just right.

"I've been expecting you two," he said with anticipation in his voice. "Guards, thank you for your service. Please leave us." The guards left the Throne Room and shut the door behind them immediately. Obviously this was going to be a very private conversation between the three of them. Zeus turned towards the two men. "I've got a lot to say to the both of you but I'll just start by saying that a spiritual death never escapes my knowledge Lord Hammond. Zeus paused for a second to let that statement sink in before continuing. "I am also well aware that the majority of spirits in this realm believe themselves to be completely immune to death. They think death is not a possibility for them simply because they've never seen it or experienced it in this realm before. I intend to keep it this way. Do you both understand?" Lord Hammond and the Reaper nodded in agreement. Zeus continued speaking. "My purpose as Lord of this realm is to help others reach their maximum potential. I want them to only focus on becoming better versions of themselves and not on all the horrible things that could still happen to them. Do you understand?" Both men nodded in agreement again.

Zeus looked directly at Lord Hammond. "There's really not a way to sugar coat what I'm about to say Lord Hammond so I'll just say it directly. I know you killed Hades. I am also aware that you completely destroyed his entire Pool of Lost Souls. In the Mortal Realm, these crimes would be cause for serious punishment! However, here in the Immortal Realm, I consider what you did to be an act of mercy." Lord Hammond looked surprised. "Why do you say that sir," he asked curiously. Zeus took a step closer towards him. "I say that because every one of those lost souls had suffered long enough for their wrong doings in mortality and it was about time someone put them out of their misery, as terrible as that may sound. There comes a time when you must ask yourself; is a lifetime of wicked behavior worth an eternity of punishment? A mortal lifetime and a spiritual eternity are very different things Lord Hammond. I also know that the only way for the lost souls to have experienced the second death is for you to have found the Krono Crystal. This is how I know you are in possession of it."

Lord Hammond was listening very carefully. "Zeus, I don't mean to interrupt but I just have to ask, what do you mean by the second death? How many deaths are there?" Zeus looked at him seriously. "The first death is commonly referred to as the mortal death. Good spirits end up here in the Immortal Realm with us. Wicked spirits end up in the Underworld inside the Pool of Lost Souls. Wicked spirits usually experience the second death. This happens after a long period of being trapped inside the Pool of Lost Souls. From there, the Lord of the Underworld has the final say as to what will happen to them. He can choose whether or not to set them free, keep them there or destroy them completely. This is why the Krono Crystal was in Hattie's possession. He could have destroyed them completely and put an end to their misery. You can only imagine what it would be like to be trapped in the Pool of Lost Souls for all eternity." Lord Hammond interjected, "I'm sure their misery is beyond my comprehension Zeus!"

Zeus continued. "Of course, there comes a time when the suffering of the wicked needs to end as well. Many centuries ago I began to regret giving Hades the final say on what happened to the Pool of Lost Souls. So I decided to take matters into my own hands." Lord Hammond seemed intrigued. "What did you do Zeus?" Zeus continued. "I went down to the Underworld in search of the Krono Crystal. I was searching for it after coming to the conclusion that it was to cruel of punishment to let the Lord of the Underworld hold onto it and possibly never use it. Unfortunately, I never found where Hades hid it and of course he wouldn't tell me. Since I couldn't find it, I decided to forge a weapon of my own that held similar qualities to the Krono Crystal. That is when I portaled myself to the top of Mount Olympus and patiently waited to catch a lightning bolt! It took a great deal of waiting and focusing but after many days of standing in the drenching rain, I finally caught the lightning bolt I had been patiently awaiting! I was finally able to forge it together with other elements from the same mountain. This is the same mountain where my father Kronos forged that dreaded Kronos Crystal! Anyways, the lightning bolt I caught is now contained within the golden staff you see me holding now. It has the power to destroy spirits as well Lord Hammond. This weapon was forged for many other reasons as well but one of them was so that I could put the Pool of Lost Souls out of their misery if I ever needed to. Hades considered death to be worse than letting his Pool of Lost Souls swim around endlessly for all eternity. I'm not really sure why. Hopefully the new Lord of the Underworld will be kinder to the wicked souls than he was."

Even though Zeus was referring to him, Lord Hammond had something else on his mind entirely. "That's incredibly intriguing," said Lord Hammond. "Although, I can't help but notice that you haven't answered my original question entirely. How many deaths are there exactly?" Zeus frowned. "Lord Hammond, this is highly confidential information. So, if I divulge such sensitive information to you then you both must promise to never tell another soul as long as you both shall live! I don't want other spirits thinking they can get away with whatever mischief they want to in this realm in hopes of simply going to another one if they decide to be a horrible person. Are we agreed?" Lord Hammond nodded in agreement. "I understand Zeus. I won't tell a soul!" The Reaper nodded his head in agreement as well.

Zeus took a deep breath as if preparing to jump into the deepest part of an ocean. "It sounds like you're wanting to know what happened to Hades and his Pool of Lost Souls after you destroyed them. Am I right Lord Hammond?" Lord Hammond nodded again. "Yes, I am wondering about that," he said seriously.

Zeus continued his explanation. "The second death happens when a spirit dies in the Immortal Realm and becomes a phantom to live in Limbo. This is a place somewhere between the Mortal and Immortal Realms. If a phantom were to somehow die in Limbo, he or she would become an earth element which would eventually be used by a God to help create a world somewhere in space. This would be considered the third death. If that element were to eventually burn up by fire on the new planet it was placed on, this would be considered the fourth death. If the ash from that element were to be blown into the ocean and then swallowed by a sea monster then that would be considered the fifth death! Assuming the sea monster were to get caught and eaten with the ash still inside it; that would be considered the sixth death. Assuming a human ate the sea monster and then died from food poisoning...this would be considered the seventh death! This is what is known as the great circle of death!"

Lord Hammond looked at Zeus with complete astonishment. "You've got to be joking! Please tell me you're joking Zeus!" Zeus looked at Lord Hammond seriously. "Okay, I'll admit...I don't actually know what happens after the third death. You'd have to talk to the Lord of Limbo to find out more about that." Lord Hammond laughed out loud! "Oh Zeus, you do have a sense of humor! You really had me going there for a second. Well done!" Zeus smiled. "Well, I have to tell a good joke every now and then or things start to get a little boring around here," he chuckled. "The truth is that life is all about spiritual progression and it was never meant for me or any other God to focus on death. Our focus should be on becoming better versions of ourselves Lord Hammond, not what would happen if we were to continue getting worse." Lord Hammond agreed.

Lord Hammond had a question that was burning him up inside. "So, what about second chances Zeus? Were the Pool of Lost Souls doomed to live in the Underworld for all eternity? If I didn't come along and destroy them with my Krono Crystal, would they have ever been given another chance in life?" Zeus looked serious again. "Those particular spirits were to wicked to be given another chance in the World of Mortals. Sadly, some spirits have the potential to drag others down to the point of never letting them progress in mortality or after that either. This is why Hades job was to hold onto them so they wouldn't be let loose in the Mortal World. This is why it is the Reaper's job to stop the wicked from ruining the spiritual progression of those in Mortal Realm. Of course I want all spirits to progress and become better versions of themselves but we also have to consider the effect that certain spirits have on others."

Zeus looked upwards for a second and continued. "No, I don't like to cut any mortal's experience short but sometimes it has to be done for the sake of letting others progress further without hindrance. It's a horrible job that I would never want to do myself but that is why the Reaper has been appointed to do it. Hades also had a job that I would never want to do as well but everyone can handle things at a different level. Everyone has their own spiritual gifts to discover no matter how strange they may be. You'd be surprised at the variety of spiritual gifts people have. These are what make people unique and special in their own way. For example, the ability to deal with and live around evil spirits without it bothering a person is definitely a gift. Hades did this every day in the Underworld," said Zeus with a bit of sadness in his voice.

Lord Hammond thought he saw a small tear run down Zeus's cheek. "Sir, are you crying?" Zeus wiped away his tear. "Yes Lord Hammond. Hades was never really my friend but his spiritual gift to live in the Underworld and deal with the high amount of evil that lived there was truly incredible! There are very few spirits living in the Immortal Realm who have that unique ability. Of course, everyone has their faults but I always try to see the good in others no matter how bad they seem to be."

Zeus walked up next to Lord Hammond and gently wrapped his right arm around his shoulders in what looked like a side hug. "You may already know this Lord Hammond but the moment you destroyed Hades was the moment you became Lord of the Underworld. All of his powers were transferred directly to you. You have probably already noticed by now that you have the ability to hover?" Lord Hammond nodded. "Yes that is true." Zeus smiled. "You have probably also noticed yourself feeling a greater sense of power and judgment over others," Lord Hammond nodded again. "Yes, that is true as well." Zeus squeezed Lord Hammond's right shoulder a bit tighter in his side embrace before letting him go. "There are many other powers you will soon discover. Just remember that you now have a responsibility to live in the Underworld and to guard the new Pool of Lost Souls that will continue to be collected by the Reaper for you. Guard them with your life! They must never be allowed to enter the Mortal Realm again," he said authoritatively. The Reaper will continue to collect those wicked souls and add them to your pool for safe keeping. In addition to guarding the Pool of Lost Souls, you are free to make negotiations with the wicked spirits who desperately want another chance in mortality. Those spirits will be ferried into

the Underworld by your skeleton ferryman. I'm sure there will
be plenty of motivational ideas you can create to help those
wicked ones become better versions of themselves. Many souls
might call you "the devil" but we both know that is not why you
are Lord of the Underworld. We both know that there are many
ways of helping others become better versions of themselves
and unfortunately that might require you to stoop to their level
at some point. This is not a gift I personally possess but as time
goes on, you will find yourself acquiring newer and greater
powers as Lord of the Underworld. You will also start doing
and saying things that you would normally never do or say."

Lord Hammond was still trying to process the fact that
he was now the Lord of the Underworld. He turned towards
Zeus. "Zeus, I don't want to do this. Please, give the job to
someone else. I beg you!" Zeus shook his head. "I'm sorry
Lord Hammond but it has been a law since the dawn of time
that he who slays the Lord of the Underworld must take his
place. This is the law and your punishment for killing Hades."
Lord Hammond looked downwards. "So, are you saying that
Hades and the Pool of Lost Souls that I destroyed are in Limbo
now?"

Zeus exhaled in a way that clearly stated he was
disappointed this whole tragedy had ever occurred. "That's
where they were headed but unfortunately something very
unexpected happened to them. Hades and the Pool of Lost
Souls were about to enter into Limbo when they were suddenly
snatched out of the sky!" A look of surprise appeared on Lord
Hammond's face. "What in the name of Hades happened to
them and who could do such a thing?"

Zeus continued. "It's kind of a long story but you
probably already know by now that there have been a long line
of Reapers who have taken the job throughout the course of

time. Each one became more power hungry than the previous one. Unfortunately, one of them, named Robin Threadbare, managed to find the Well of Souls inside the Mortal Realm. The Well of Souls was originally used as a fixed portal to get in and out of the Underworld. Unfortunately, many evil spirits began to escape out of the Underworld and into the Mortal Realm through it. So, Hades made a decision to close it off forever at the time. Sadly, Robin opened it again. It has remained open ever since. So, when you used the Krono Crystal to destroy Hades and The Pool of Lost Souls, they all attempted to escape the Underworld through the Well of Souls instead of being sucked into Limbo where they should have gone. The only catch is that Robin had a Collector's Jar waiting to catch them at the top of the well."

"What exactly is a Collector's Jar," Lord Hammond asked curiously. Zeus looked up into the air and began stroking his long white beard thoughtfully. "Simply put, it's a special glass jar used to collect evil spirits. Anciently, they were used by Reapers to collect wicked souls and bring them to the Pool of Lost Souls in the Underworld. Eventually, Reapers stopped using them and started using various crystals instead. A crystal is much more convenient to carry around and can easily be attached to the inside of a scythe blade. Now days, a Reaper will collect evil spirits using Bloodstones instead of Collector's Jars. Anyways, I've gotten off track from my original story. What was I talking about before?" Lord Hammond interjected, "um, you were talking about how Robin Threadbare collected the spirits of Hades and the other Lost Souls inside the Collector's Jar." "Oh, that's right," said Zeus with a laugh. "I'm glad you have been paying attention Lord Hammond." Zeus looked towards the Reaper standing next to Lord Hammond. "I know much of this is probably just a history lesson for you Reaper but if you pay attention, you might learn a few things too." The Reaper nodded silently.

Zeus continued. "To make a long story short, the former Reaper Robin Threadbare has collected the spirits of Hades and the entire Pool of Lost Souls inside her Collector's Jar and is probably going to use them to start a revolution against me!" "Wait a second," said Lord Hammond. "Robin Threadbare is a woman? Doesn't that go against the Reaper Rules or something like that?" Zeus slapped the palm of his hand against his forehead. "No, it doesn't. Although, I must say that it was Hades who recommended her for the job. He convinced me that she could be just as good of a Reaper as anyone else. Well, sufficed to say, she only lasted two days as Reaper before she got herself into some major trouble!" Lord Hammond and the Reaper standing next to him both seemed on edge for more information. "What did she do that was so bad," Lord Hammond asked curiously.

Zeus scanned the room quickly before continuing just to make sure unwanted listeners weren't within ear shot. Zeus leaned in towards the two men and his voice became extremely quiet before continuing...."She found the Key to Limbo!" Lord Hammond couldn't control his excitement! He began coughing as if he had just choked on something huge. "Whoa...that just opened up a whole new world for me Zeus! I didn't know Limbo actually existed until today! What is the purpose of this place anyways?"

Zeus continued speaking, "remember this needs to stay confidential. Do you understand?" The Reaper nodded agreeably and Lord Hammond chimed in with, "don't worry Zeus! Your secret is safe with me. Please, go on..."

Zeus looked happy for the agreement of confidentiality and continued. "I created Limbo as a safe haven for evil spirits who had enough courage to escape their fate in the Underworld. Remember, I don't believe that wicked souls should suffer in the Underworld forever. So, I created three portals going in and out of Limbo. One of them is located between where the ferryman docks his ferry and where he drops the evil souls off in the Underworld. Often times, evil souls will jump off the ferry in an attempt to escape their fates. This is what the Kraken is for. The Kraken is a giant squid like sea monster that will follow the ferry into the Underworld and snatch up any soul who jumps overboard. It's long tentacles will wrap around the person's body and throw him or her back on board the ferry where he or she belongs. However, there are a lucky few who end up swimming down far enough to where Limbo's portal is located. If a person is lucky enough to get passed the Kraken and find the portal to Limbo, they will stay there until they are lucky enough to find one of the other two portals leading out of that dreaded place. Of course, they could use the same portal to get back out but the Kraken would still be there waiting for them. Limbo is basically a long mazed labyrinth that could take multiple lifetimes to escape. On the bright side, it's still a mercy to the ones brave enough to escape their fate in the Underworld."

Lord Hammond and the Reaper were taking in all this new information with great astonishment and amazement! "So where are the other two portals leading in and out of Limbo," Lord Hammond asked curiously." Zeus shook his head. "Unfortunately, I will have to keep that information a closely guarded secret for now. There are to many unfortunate souls still in Limbo who are still looking for a way out. However, keep in mind that they are still better off there than in the Underworld where they were originally headed in the first place."

Lord Hammond had a question. "So, why did the former Reaper, Robin Threadbare, lose her Reaper position for finding a key to Limbo? Also, I didn't know any portal in existence had a key to it." Zeus continued his story. "The three portals going in and out of Limbo are of such great importance that I had to have keys made for two of them. The third one didn't need a key since it is guarded by the Kraken. I won't tell you where the other two portals are located exactly but I will say that the key Robin found to Limbo was located inside the Mortal Realm. It is important that only the right people know where the keys can be found otherwise an entire army of souls could be set free from Limbo!"

It had been a long time since the Reaper had said anything at all but he decided the moment was right to do so. "How would a spirit escape from Limbo without a key?" Zeus looked at the Reaper. "That's an excellent question Reaper. You always know the most relevant questions to ask. There are multiple keys hidden all throughout Limbo. A soul must find one of them along with its correct portal to escape. The real problem is what people do with their keys once they leave Limbo. Many will hold onto their keys for safe keeping while others will just toss them aside only for others to come along and find later. Eventually, Robin found one of those keys in the Mortal Realm that had been tossed aside and unlocked a Limbo Portal. Obviously, this made it much easier for evil spirits to escape but it also made it easier for mortals to get into Limbo as well!" Lord Hammond gasped loudly! He could see where this story was heading and he didn't like it one bit.

Zeus continued. "As you can imagine, once Robin Threadbare opened the portal to Limbo, many evil spirits escaped back into the Mortal Realm. Not only that, but mortals have found their way into Limbo as well! This has created some major problems! First of all, there are still mortals lurking around in Limbo as we speak! Second of all, a certain mortal who found the open portal started showing other mortals where it was located and even decided to try and make a living by doing so. It's pretty ridiculous how far some mortals will go to make money but since we don't use money here in the Immortal Realm, I can't judge him to harshly. He goes by the name of Todd Fisher just in case you were wondering. As you can imagine, this is causing problems for people in all realms. That being said, I'm going to need William to round up another team to go find all the lost mortals in Limbo and get them out of there! They don't belong there and they definitely shouldn't be there. Speaking of which, where is good old William anyways?"

Lord Hammond looked at the Reaper and then back towards Zeus. "He is inside the giant's lair searching for his staff at the moment. Jimbo and Rooster are both searching with him as well." Zeus started walking away from them. "Alright, let's go find them before they get into any serious trouble. But I'm just going to summarize a few things before we do. Lord Hammond, you are now Lord of the Underworld. It is now your duty to protect the Krono Crystal and to only use it when necessary. You must also keep the Pool of Lost Souls safe as the Reaper continues to fill it with wicked spirits. Hades and the Pool of Lost Souls are currently trapped inside a Collector's Jar being held by the former Reaper Robin Threadbare. The door to Limbo is now open inside the Mortal Realm and Todd Fisher is selling tickets for others to see it."

Zeus turned towards the Reaper. "I know it's a lot to take in but I want you to continue your duties as Reaper until I can find a decent replacement for you. I am aware that the position of Reaper can grow a bit tiresome even for the strongest of spirits. This is why I am always on the lookout for new Reapers. Unfortunately, it takes a special kind of spirit to fill this position. Not just anyone can do what you do Reaper." For the first time in the Reaper's existence, he felt completely flattered and appreciated by Zeus. "Thank you sir," he said in his deep mystical and crackly voice. Zeus smiled. "That being said, I want to know what is going on with you collecting innocent spirits before their time has expired in mortality. Why have you been doing such a thing?"

The Reaper looked at Zeus, his red eyes gleaming beneath his dark hood. "My Collector's Clock is missing," he said mystically. Zeus gazed upwards for a moment as if contemplating. "Well, that would explain a lot. You obviously wouldn't know when someone's mortal clock has expired unless you had your Collectors Clock with you. Do you have any idea where it might have gone Reaper?" The Reaper looked downwards at the shiny marble floor beneath them. "Hades borrowed it for an experiment and never returned it," he said as if confessing to a deeply held secret.

"And what kind of experiment would that be," Zeus asked curiously. Lord Hammond lowered his head, shocked at how well Zeus had just taken that bit of information. The Reaper continued staring downwards as if trying to avoid Zeus's gaze. "Hades wanted to use the Collectors Clock on the Pool of Lost Souls to see if they truly were doomed to swim in the pool for all eternity! He never gave the clock back to me and I never found out the answer," said the Reaper with dismay in his voice. Lord Hammond began thinking about what Morpheus had told him about why Hades had confiscated the Reaper's Collectors Clock. He had said "it was so that the Reaper could collect innocent souls without breaking Reaper Ruler number four." Lord Hammond didn't know for sure who was telling the truth but he didn't want to get the Reaper in trouble so he avoided mentioning his thoughts about Morpheus to Zeus at the moment.

Zeus frowned at the Reaper. "He should have told you the Pool of Lost Souls are doomed to stay in the Underworld for all eternity unless someone were to destroy them or set them free. However, the real problem we are facing now is that Hades was destroyed while holding onto your Collectors Clock and his spirit is now trapped inside Robin's Collectors Jar along with thousands of other lost souls.

Zeus turned to face the Reaper. "Unfortunately, without your Collectors Clock, it will be nearly impossible for you to perform all of your duties as Reaper. Thus, I hereby relieve you of your duties until we get your Collectors Clock back from Hades. This will be an incredibly difficult task to locate Robin Threadbare and her Collectors Jar. However, the first thing we need to do is pay William and his crew a visit." That being said, Zeus pointed his long golden staff towards the middle of the room. Immediately a bright flash of white light emitted from it and formed a large swirling vortex. "Let's get a move on," he said with enthusiasm. Lord Hammond and the Reaper entered the portal first. Zeus quickly followed and within seconds the swirling white portal vanished behind them.

CHAPTER 16

RETURN OF THE GIANTS

William, Rooster and Jimbo had been looking around the giant's lair for hours and couldn't seem to find the staff anywhere. They were about to give up when they heard a deep giant's voice yell out, "hey fellers, look what I found! I think we've found our prisoner again! Oh, Lord Tidus is going to be so happy with us!" It didn't take long before their little group was surrounded by the few giants who had lagged behind instead of searching of Lord Tidus as promised. "Why can't these pesky giants ever do as they're told," William thought to himself quietly.

The giants held their large wooden clubs in front of them threateningly. Rooster and Jimbo were ready to defend William with their scythes. One of the giants yelled, "not so tough without your little Reaper friend here to defend you are you?!" Just as the giants started closing in on the little group, a flash of white light appeared just behind them. They turned around to see a white swirling vortex appear out of thin air. Lord Hammond, the Reaper and Zeus himself stepped out! It didn't take long for the giants to drop their weapons and bow before Zeus. "We are deeply sorry if we have offended you in anyway your grace," said the giant spokesman. "We were only following orders from our leader Lord Tidus." Zeus began to speak authoritatively. "I want you all to go find Lord Tidus and bring him to me. There are many things we need to discuss. Go now before my temper begins to flare up!" The four giants hopped up from their bowed positions on the floor and ran towards the nearest exit.

Zeus looked at the little group. "Are you three okay?" William was shocked to see such a powerful group of people all standing right in front of him! "We are fine Zeus. Thanks for asking. Unfortunately though, I'm still not able to find my staff that contains the Fires of Avalon." Zeus stepped forward to put a hand on William's shoulder. "The Fires of Avalon is simply a flexible portal contained in a staff William. I will provide you with another flexible portal if you accept the mission I am about to send you on." William's curiosity became peaked. He had barely even finished this quest and now Zeus wanted to send him on another one. "What kind of adventure did you have in mind Zeus," he asked curiously.

Lord Hammond cut Zeus short before he could say anything. "With all due respect your Lordship, me and the Reaper would like to take our leave now. We are fully aware of the quest you are about to send William on and as newly appointed Lord of the Underworld, I would like to take some time to explore my new domain. Also, I'm sure the Reaper would like to enjoy the brief time off from his duties for a while." Zeus smiled and waved his right hand in their direction. "It has been a pleasure gentlemen. Just remember, William here will probably visit you both very soon. After all, he'll need you both when he enters into Limbo!" A look of shock and horror came over William's face. "Wait a second, Limbo actually exists? Also, why would you want to send me there?"

Lord Hammond took this as his cue to leave. He stomped his scythe on the ground three times before a dark swirling vortex appeared in front of him. "Come with me Reaper. I want to discuss a few things with you." The Reaper followed Lord Hammond through his portal and into the Underworld where they were headed. The portal disappeared behind them almost as quickly as it had appeared. Zeus continued to tell William, Jimbo and Rooster everything he had recently told Lord Hammond and the Reaper. They continued to listen with amazement and awe. After all, it wasn't every day that Zeus personally sent someone on a quest. William quickly accepted the responsibility of finding Robin Threadbare and her Collectors Jar which held Hades and thousands of other lost souls trapped inside it. It would be a long journey and it would take some brave volunteers. Of course, Jimbo and Rooster were willing and eager to travel with William. They were adventures at heart and couldn't wait to get started.

CHAPTER 17

NEW FOUND POWERS

The Reaper and Lord Hammond stepped out of the dark swirling portal that had brought them into the Underworld. It was much darker than normal without the Pool of Lost Souls to help light the cavern. Although, the first thing Lord Hammond noticed upon arriving was that his body was engulfed in blue flames just like Hades had once been. The flames did not burn him. Instead, they lit the way around him so that he could better see his way around the dark Underworld in which he now found himself. "Looks like my new powers are already beginning to take effect," he thought to himself. His entire body also felt much more powerful than normal. It was as if the place itself gave him some sort of energy boost that he couldn't explain. He felt as if he could do just about anything and everything.

Suddenly a deep mystical voice began speaking inside his mind. "Welcome back master! I hope you had a safe trip. Don't worry about speaking out loud right now. You don't need to tell the Reaper of my existence but I should tell you that he is currently hiding William's staff beneath his cloak. Use this to your advantage master! Tell the Reaper you won't reveal his little secret if he helps you create a portal into Limbo! Think about it, you don't want to be Lord of the Underworld forever. Create an escape portal for your Pool of Lost Souls to go once they get here. Then you can tell Zeus that all of your lost souls somehow managed to escape from the Underworld. That should be a good enough reason to get you off the hook from being Lord of the Underworld forever! Then you can go back to normal life in the Immortal Realm doing whatever you wish, not having any worries at all!" Lord Hammond palmed his forehead and began thinking to himself. "You're a genius Morpheus! I will do that but first I want to try out my new powers as Lord of the Underworld just to see what I can do."

He pointed the blade of his scythe towards the darkness and imagined a long row of brightly lit torches appearing in front of him. As soon as the image was in his mind, he commanded it to happen. Without delay, a bright streak of light streamed from his glowing blue scythe and the row of brightly lit torches appeared in front of him just as he had pictured in his mind! He turned to look at the Reaper. "Wow! This kind of power could really come in handy!" He tried imagining a small pond of bright red magma appearing next to him. Without even trying, the light came from his scythe and caused the small pond of magma to appear just as he had hoped.

Lord Hammond laughed out loud. "This could be fun! I mean, who says the Underworld has to be dark and gloomy all the time right? I could cover this place with brightly lit jack o' lanterns or even glowing pink bunnies for that matter but what kind of message would that be sending to all the evil doers that come here? No, I should probably portray the message that this is a serious place and the spirits who come here should take it seriously if they ever want to leave. And speaking of leaving this place….don't think I don't know about your little secret Reaper! I am fully aware that you are currently in possession of the Fires of Avalon staff that William is searching for. I simply didn't say anything to Zeus because I have my own plans for the staff as well. If you don't want Zeus to find out about your little secret then I suggest you do as I say Reaper. Don't worry, I won't be asking you to do anything horrible."

Lord Hammond looked around at his new place of residence before continuing. "Just between me and you Reaper, I don't want to be Lord of the Underworld forever. Nope, I have an escape plan that will get me out of this horrible job. I hope you're paying attention because here it is…I want you to use your Fires of Avalon to create a portal directly between the Underworld and Limbo. This way, all those in the Underworld will "accidently" find the portal into Limbo and with any luck, Zeus will fire me as Lord of the Underworld! Then I can get back to living my normal life in the Immortal Realm. It's really a win-win for everyone, including the wicked ones that want to get out of here." The Reaper nodded silently.

Lord Hammond continued speaking. "The only problem is that we can't just portal into a place we've never been to before. We're going to have to enter Limbo before we can set up a direct portal going from here to there. That being said, I want you to go on that journey with William and his group when they leave. You don't have to be a part of their group or anything. Just follow them as closely as possible until you find a way into Limbo. From there, we can create a portal going directly from here to there. Does that make sense Reaper?" The Reaper simply nodded his hooded head again.

Lord Hammond looked up at him hovering in the air. "I like you Reaper. You're always so quiet and never argue with me at all. Also, you don't have to worry about your Reaper duties at the moment like Zeus was saying. So, that should give you some free time to track William's group when they decide to set off on their journey. Is there anything I can do to help prepare you for that? You've been a great help to me by the way! Thank you for all that you've done so far." The Reaper began speaking in his deep and mystical voice. "Don't worry about me Lord Hammond. William's group won't even know I'm there. Also, be careful how you use your new found powers! They may come back to haunt you." With that, the Reaper turned away from Lord Hammond, made his portal appear and disappeared through it before Lord Hammond had a chance to say anything else to him.

CHAPTER 18

INSIDE LIMBO

A dark vortex appeared on top of a sunlit hill overlooking a giant labyrinth of trees and shrubbery. Hovering out of his portal, the Reaper threw his long bladed scythe over his shoulder and gazed downwards at the many lost souls making their way through the giant maze of trees and shrubs in an attempt to finally escape Limbo! Hades had told him that all of the innocent souls he had collected for him were going to end up here at some point. Perhaps they were down there somewhere? He wasn't exactly sure what Hades had done with them.

In any case, this was not his first time here, that was for certain. This is why he could portal into Limbo so easily. Lucky for him, Lord Hammond had no idea where he had been in his life. Otherwise, he would have commanded the Reaper to portal him directly into Limbo instead of sending him on a quest to find it. (After all, a person couldn't portal into a place they've never been to before.) He was also fortunate to have The Fires of Avalon staff in his possession. With a little ingenuity, the Reaper had figured out a way to hide the long staff within the long hollow pole of his scythe! This made it possible for him to use both of their powers without having to carry each object separately. It truly was a genius idea and he was glad to have thought of it! He was also happy to know that Zeus seemed to be completely unaware that The Fires of Avalon staff could create a direct portal into Limbo if one had been there before. It was true that a person could only enter Limbo using one of the three hidden portals that Zeus had created. However, no one seemed to know that the Reaper had already accomplished this feat many centuries ago!

Next to his portal stood a dead tree with low hanging branches; a small golden bell hung from one of the branches. The Reaper reached a bony hand out to ring it. The sound was dull but still high pitched. Almost instantly another portal appeared next to his own. A dark hooded figure with a long bladed scythe hovered out of the vortex next to him and quickly began addressing him. "I'm glad you've come Morpheus," said a female voice from beneath her hood. The Reaper continued staring downwards at the thousands of lost souls below him, trying to make their way out of the labyrinth. It disturbed him that no one in either realm had ever bothered to learn his name. Even Lord Hammond didn't know his name before making him the Reaper. All he had said was, "your previous name doesn't matter now because from here on out, you shall be known as….the Reaper." Morpheus turned towards Robin. "The plan is going just as expected! We've got a lot to talk about!"

EPILOGUE

I've finally made it back to my home here in the Immortal Realm. Looks like I'll be going on another quest soon. William agreed to Zeus's request. He'll be getting another group of spirits together soon to venture into Limbo. We'll be trying to round up a large number of mortals who have found their way there. They will need to be escorted back into the Mortal Realm as soon as possible. Heaven knows they wouldn't be able to make it back without our help. Apparently, Limbo is a giant labyrinth filled with all sorts of traps and monsters most people have never seen before. I can only hope the mortals trapped there have not all been killed off by now. Zeus claims they are a lot tougher than they look so that gives me some hope for them.

Considering there are only three portals in and out of Limbo, we must be extremely careful trying to find them. One of those portals is guarded by the Kraken so we probably won't be using that one. The other two portals are extremely hard to find and actually have keys to them that need to be found before entering. Zeus put the two portals and their keys in places that are not easily accessible for mortals or immortals alike. He says that Limbo was never meant to be a crowded place and that mortals were never supposed to find their way into it! However, since this seems to be the case; we prepare ourselves for another long journey.

Zeus provided William with another staff containing a flexible portal. Unfortunately, we can't simply portal into a place we've never been to before so we are going to have to search it out first. Unfortunately, Zeus won't be able to provide a portal for us to get into Limbo even though he has been there before. He claims the only way in and out is to use one of the three hidden portals and that even a flexible portal isn't going to work in this case. Even then, finding the correct keys will be an adventure all by itself! Portal travel seems to be much more complex than I ever thought it would be but that's only because most of us here in the Immortal Realm are used to using fixed portals only. I guess us travelers are starting to learn the difference between fixed, flexible and locked portals. Apparently, they all have their own special rules that need to be followed in order for them to work correctly. I think we are getting the hang of it rather quickly though.

It would seem that Lord Hammond is now the new Lord of the Underworld and the Reaper is no longer performing his duties since his Collector's Clock was stolen by Hades. They will probably go on a separate journey to find Hades and the Collector's Clock. In the meantime, there will be a lot of dying souls in the Mortal Realm who won't be able to go to the Underworld since the Reaper is currently out of a job! What does this mean for them? Well, it means that their wicked spirits will remain trapped inside their dead mortal bodies until another Reaper has been validated by Zeus to come along and collect them for the Pool of Lost Souls. Either outcome is a tragedy but at least all the wicked ones will one day be together, floating around endlessly in a pool of misery and despair! At least they'll all have each-other to talk to about how miserable they are…and that's better than nothing, right?!

Also, it would seem that Lord Hammond doesn't want to be Lord of the Underworld forever so he will probably go in search of Hades who was captured by the former Reaper, Robin Threadbare, inside her Collectors Jar. There is a good chance she is hiding out in Limbo and possibly building an army there in hopes of one day waging war against Zeus himself!

There was once a time when I felt that the Immortal Realm was a safe and secure place to live. However, simply knowing that Lord Hammond is now in possession of a weapon so deadly it could destroy even a spirit….is a bit concerning to me! We can only hope that he will continue to stay a good person and not give in to the enticing dark powers of the Underworld. His new found powers might make him feel invincible and perhaps he will want to take control of the entire Immortal Realm one day just like many others before him have wanted as well. The worst thing he could do now would be to join forces with Robin Threadbare! Let's hope things don't turn in that direction but I can only record things as they happen.

If you are a mortal reading this diary right now, I can only hope that the entire Immortal Realm has not been taken over by an army of lost souls by now! Of course, this is all just information and might not mean much to you mortals….until you die of course!

Yours Truly,

Jimbo Jenkins the 3rd

ABOUT THE AUTHOR

J.R. Carlson loves to write fantasy novels for your enjoyment. He would enjoy hearing from his readers. If you enjoyed this book, please write to him at AuthorJ.R.Carlson@gmail.com.

www.ingramcontent.com/pod-product-compliance
Lightning Source LLC
Chambersburg PA
CBHW030534130626
46552CB00006B/2259